FILLED

WITH

GHOSTS

KAREN LITTLE

T0315973

Onion Custard Publishing Ltd

Filled With Ghosts

© Karen Little

13 Ways of Looking at Beetles was previously published in Lockjaw
magazine, Bully was previously published in Here Comes Everything
Magazine, and the poetry heading the four sections was previously published
as Serrato in Bunbury E-zine.

British Library Cataloguing in Publication Data. A catalogue record for this
book is available from the British Library.

Published in the United Kingdom by Onion Custard Publishing Ltd.
www.onioncustard.com
Twitter @onioncustard
Facebook.com/OnionCustardPublishing

Paperback: ISBN: 9781909129771

First Edition: December, 2015
Category: Contemporary Women's Fiction

For my son, Pascal,
and the furbabies,
Skelly, Noodles, and Chicken

Acknowledgements

To anyone who has ever rescued an animal and shown it love. All my friends on Platt Fields who walk their dogs tell me their stories and listen to mine. The many people not on this list who have been amazing, friendly, and even helped me to get my poetry and prose out there.

Anyone named below has done a weird mix that could include anything from: saving my life; saving my computer; making me frequently laugh out loud; being kind and supportive; reading the first draft of my novella; to showing support for its final incarnation.

Ailsa Abraham, Adam Prince, Alex Klineberg, Amina Lesley Mottley, Anna and Becca at *Stirred*, Andrew Lawson, Angela Readman, Batzilla, Carly Bennett, Carol Robson, Cathy Thomas-Bryant, Christopher Moriarty, Daniel Parsons, David Evans, David Norrington, Eve Arroyo, Fidel Foley-Little, Fiona Pitt-kethley, Gavyn Japp, Gina Frost and John at *3MT*, Hannah Jayne Louise Brimson, Hayley, Ian Little, Jackie Hagan, Jane Leek-Kelly, Jane Thrace, Janus Richard Avivson, Jean and Sunny, John G. Hall, Joshua Mackle, Joshua Williams, Kate Bush, Keir Thomas-Bryant, Keri-Ann Edwards, Larry Foley-Little, Laura H. Lockington, Linda Foley-Little, Lorraine Beckett-Murray, Matt Panesh, Matthew P. Lomas, Maureen Little, Maureen Lynch, Melissa Lee-Houghton, Midnight Shelley, Mike Heath, Ollie Hiatt, Paul Tristram, Pascal Little, Pascale Petit, Peta Lily, Rhys Milsom, Rosie Garland, Ruth Clemens, Sarah L. Dixon, Steffeny McGiffen, Stephanie Portersmith, Steve Lyons, Sue Barnard, Taslima Ahmad, Tony Kasazkaja, Vinny Foley-Little, and Wendy Pratt.

PART ONE

On a dusty path, the hind leg of a dog lies exposed as figs fall heavily. Featherless birds drop from beak-drilled holes in dried mud banks, and shotgun shells are scattered in red, blue, and green abandon.

Diana

Miguel flaunts his money, marriage, and newborn son. I let him climb into my bed, because it's what I've done for fifteen years. Every morning, I build sentences from my own spit, bare words gobbed from raw lips. Ill-fitting windows let in a train's phallic smoke, sticking it in, battering my eyes. I trip on the edge of anger as the neighbours' collective whining rattles tins and carelessly hacks open the day. Scraps of bacon, cold fat, egged plates, lie between me and a narrow bathtub, ringed with shaving-cream scum. Another night of excess, written up as fictional shock. I am rubble. I am not worth grooming.

Shedding corpuscles, I trip memory's switch, a risky procedure leading to the circulation of misery. Am I the same girl whose bare-arsed handstands had teachers rising? Who languidly dragged on a cigarette, while the fire alarms screamed, leaving her friends to dance before the firing squad like cooked spaghetti? From underneath covers smelling of feet, puppy, and sulphur-tipped breath, the dough of Miguel's face rises in jelly-coloured light.

* * *

I love the damp forest floor. I step over a transparent yellow sweet wrapper – a clue that someone has recently walked ahead. Only the treetops are swaying, while the ferns fold their white edges into tiny cigarettes. We're smoking too, just to keep the insects at bay.

When we reach a familiar boulder, Miguel finally throws down his defences and we lie amongst pencil-thin quilled trunks, the tree's barbs making them appear as plucked as chickens.

I feel the silence, it's so quiet I can hear the insects bite. As usual, I'm trusting hemp oil and lavender, but midges enter my eye, the one organ that can't be defended. We watch a dog shake off unwelcome emotion. I pull back the edges of the dripping fern, revealing strangely coloured plants, and I say, "It's like looking into a fish tank," and Miguel says, "You killed my fish, it's much worse than planticide." We both know I can kill plants just by looking at them.

I feed him peppery nasturtiums, and pick mushrooms from the forest floor, damp now because the dry and sticky summer's almost history. I lead him to where the cascade is longest and rushes louder than the hammering of my hurting heart.

I say "Let's lie down here. The long grass is lush. The short grass would scratch our skin."

Miguel pulls away from me, trampling his own path, but then decides, "You can help me today if you work carefully."

I settle on a leather coat, my feet resting on the rock of him.

"Miguel, I think I can smell the sea. I want you to react like seaweed. I don't mean describe it. I want you to slip like seaweed through my fingers."

"Dee, you can't smell the sea, it's too far away. What you smell is the mackerel salad."

I refuse to be disappointed. Miguel has always been the pounding water, and I the wet poncho he throws off when he decides to risk rain rather than feel enclosed. Fifteen years and a child together, but he has never given me commitment. I taste his sweat, and tell him, "You're like sugar on apple cake."

But he says "That can't be right. Catalina tells me I'm salty."

"Are you saying she has the more sensitive tongue?"

"Dee, Catalina's money will solve all our problems. You and I are still together, even though I moved my things into Catalina's villa."

"You don't see why I'm bothered about you marrying Catalina, do you?"

I turn my head away from Miguel's confident smile and throw up the mackerel I was eating. The greasy hideousness of the fish and its glassy eyes. Mackerel will hereafter join the smells that represent repulsion and sickness, and the ills of the world.

We're passing through the tackiness of pine forests, past the deep, dry well, the abandoned beehives rotting, towards the desert of cowboy country. Miguel leads me to a place for lovers. He whispers he's hollow, his heart scooped out by the squirrels.

"Is it surprising a gang of squirrels can tear a dog apart when there are no winter nuts? Starving, we're all at our fiercest, but also our most beautiful, our most free."

He sniffs the air, trying to hunt down an elusive wind-carried odour. Some sounds are ceaseless, they whisper like nubs of cloth woven into the silence. Sounds that seem to come from behind. Miguel drops onto his belly to warm it on the ground.

He pulls me down next to him, and I realise we're spying on a gay couple. They're so attentive to each other, the boy seeming to hang on every word the older man says, so tactile I am mesmerised by them.

When we approach, they offer to share their food with us, and the boy runs to their car to bring wine and plums.

I watch as Miguel wraps a handkerchief around the aft of his knife, and quickly slips it into the man's flesh. What made him give in to fantasy, why couldn't he resist carrying it out this time? My brain registers the fact that maybe he has never resisted, that the photos Miguel doesn't even bother to hide from me are more than theatrical tableau.

Have I been in denial for years?

The boy stumbles carrying back the drawstring bag, and one of the bottles it contains smashes on the rocky ground. It drips a deep red that is quickly lost among the brighter red already soaking through his boyfriend's cheesecloth shirt. The boy, hand on hip, can't believe the man is biting earth, like the lolly whose wooden stick is still gripped in his hand. The transparent red sugar lolly smashes so beautifully when it hits the ground.

The man lies crumpled, redundant.

Miguel quickly slips the knife into the boy's neck, and twists, before returning it to his belt. My eyes are fuzzy as I watch Miguel hold aloft, and then drink from, a strangely-spouted amber bottle, one of the couple's souvenirs from the drawstring bag. Miguel laughs as he stamps the ground, clicks imaginary castanets, and grins an 'Ole!' Everything split open like a soggy parcel, and I look in disbelief at the spilled contents.

A stench rapidly covers everything.

Miguel says "Dee, you look so sexy in your yellow hot pants with that tiny bib. The perfect picture."

I'm horrified. The dead strangers are still smiling, though they see nothing. I fall over, just before Miguel takes the photo. We should've made it to the desert.

I feel wasted, all bones, as I press myself into the dusty leather driving seat of the car, my clothes still scented with rich wild herbs; mint, sage, thyme, and lavender, released when we dragged the heavy bodies into hiding. Miguel wants to keep their *Volkswagen Beetle* as a souvenir, but of course I'll abandon it.

I ask what happens if the bodies are found and Miguel says, "Nothing."

I whisper he's barking policeman mad. I tell him I need solitude, to allow my thoughts their quiet rummage and assembly.

As I drive, I see the heat bake the road ahead, a rainbow hovering in the high pass, cracking open the defences of this giant mountain range. It's the most incredible sky when rain clears toward evening. Filled with ghosts.

* * *

In my dream I watch myself cutting off my own left hand at the wrist, and then the elbow, with a huge knife. It's totally painless. I see a vein bulge and wonder why it's painless. When I've done it I say, "That was stupid. That's the hand I draw and paint with."

I can see the whole of the mapping I've been painting onto doors and corrugated metal roofs. The image is endless, but I see it all connected, as if I am flying or scrolling over it. It makes huge sense.

There's no recourse, no way to disavow the crime. It lies here, a solid mistake, like a tongue, all muscle. A dead weight that can't reach into the corners. I feel crushed by every sound, taken over by aches, and floundering. I wish I could wander off, separate, leaving a gap Miguel can't catch onto. I won't let Miguel near me, he is staying at Catalina's, but crept into our home and left a message under the fridge magnet.

Dee,

There's a blue so dangerous the Greeks have always worshipped it, and made sacrifices in its honour. I've seen lips and feet this colour, but not at the same time. One blue brought death and the other, the beginning of life. Both are fragments of the circle we recognise as Time. Does it make a difference if you believe these people will go to a better place? That perhaps they'll be shown the way to a better life?

Dee, life without you is dull and blunt.

I am yours,

Miguel

Outside the window a vine grows and strangles everything. Knowing what we did horrifies and shames me. I drop a pin down the bottomless well, but as fragile as it is, I imagine I hear it hit the bottom, after bouncing off the sides.

I hear the cream rise in the milk, the rug sigh when my feet pass over it. I hear my own eyelashes rustle, and unexpectedly experience a sudden and awful sensitivity to light that has me yearning to hide.

A mouse has died somewhere in this room. I sense small bones crammed into a hole the size of a twenty pence piece, the rug groaning with the crack of a centipede's back.

New resolve cuts through me as precise as surgery. It's time to sew back my severed artist's hands, shrink-wrapped to preserve their impossible drive.

Miguel

I love vodka, it tastes cold and empty, the solitude of unanswered prayers. I hate the warmth of frothy beer, its bonhomie, fake gladness. I accept we're all alone, glacially cold, on a polar bear hunt with cracking ice, and only a fishing pole assists us in this frozen wasteland of our own devising. Tonight, drug withdrawal has me heaving. I'm a pierced, raw lump of red meat healing slowly, rolled around in my own drool and vomit. I must take a breath.

My young daughter would always watch me, bug-eyed as I put in the spike, blazing drugs which wrapped me round tree trunks, tasting the breeze, smelling the inside of clouds, teasing waves, scaling cliffs. Nothing was ever enough.

It is fifteen years since Dee tried to rescue me from vodka on cornflakes; from drunk in a ditch, and joined me in my mother's derelict house of snatched purses and smoky hell.

In return I held her while she waited for the last of the candles to hiss into the bottom of wine bottles. I watched her eyeballs when she couldn't sleep. I encouraged her to stay awake for days on end, and fight normality with me. I told her 'Things aren't what they seem.' She said 'Things are exactly as they seem.'

That first night I told her, "I'll melt you like oil on sugar," and she let me, writing our story on playing cards. A story I gambled away on street corners and in drug dens. I crashed her opening, took her fever without asking for it. Touching her was to unfold an envelope filled with seeds she spilled everywhere.

After that first time, she often came to look for me between awake and nightmare. She called me a vagabond, a romantic word for someone without fixed abode often begging to survive. *Vagabond*, (like *swashbuckling*, or *abscond*) is a word she savours. It taps at her skull, asking to be used in the repository of her work. I tell her she's a nostalgic pornographer, and I deliberately hit a nerve, knowing her paintings aren't a desire to awaken the past, but an attempt to put it to rest, so she can move forward. She says 'I'm not the only person who wakes up and pieces myself together before I can even make the coffee!'

One thing had to be resolved between us: I require my women to keep their breathing quiet and hold back their pleasure. If they let go too soon it's a wasted opportunity. We need to conform to more than five senses, let ourselves feel more. Dee puts herself into my hands as I carve away at her skin, cut through membrane, cut through the veil, tread on the toes of death. We see things differently, walk with our mind, and hover around asphyxiation, without even the security of a lemon slice between the teeth. Split-second timing and rare trust stretch our minds: we rely on each other to unbuckle the belt in time, to keep us alive. We get there in the end, find another way of being, and it binds us more than black does absence of light. In our states of calmest death we hold colour in the palm of our hands, pulsing on the edge of concave, on the corner of convex.

"Miguel, how can we ever end? Who else needs this like we do?"

"I'll help myself to a feast of you, and if you stop offering I'll take you down."

Pilar

Is good to have family live with me, and hard when they split up. Suddenly Dee want more time to make her art. I don't say anything against Miguel, but Dee probably more caring person.

He humiliate people, try to control them, even as teenager. Miguel convince local kids enter my shed, get naked, use nettles to lash them. Their crime – they have fathers – and his die. When I catch him I have fit, but no way to control him.

Now he spend money on drink and drugs, get lazy, make Heena do labelling and bottling of medicines. He think the women attract by him, and sure, he good looking like his father.

Miguel not so clever though.

Fourteen years old he get first conviction for thieving, land up in reformatory school. He get into fight and need hospital treatment. When he start to get better, doctors use him take drinks and medicine to patients, do all kinds of work. Authorities want him back in reformatory, but doctors say he still need treatment, and keep him another month. While he in hospital, his father get drunk and hit head on kerb. Dies. Miguel never admit how he die, he invent heroic act to explain father's death.

I just complete ninth model-kit ship. Take five weeks and I build like shipbuilder, in right order, right up to final fitting. Sergio not go near model; he afraid of yellow rust on ship, and he even think about shipwreck make him sick.

This model my favourite ship because of story

attached. In war, Captain sail it once, then keep in harbour, say it need rudder repair. Meanwhile, visit local bars with crew every night, get totally smashed. He say he patrolling harbour, but never do. Eventually he called to task. They discover nothing wrong with ship. Captain refuse go to sea again, and ship in harbour five week until someone take over to re-join battle. Captain hang boots above bar and settle himself in front of fire.

I identify with Captain because I know what is to stray from path. I many years a drug mule, is how I put food in children's mouths, my husband never provide. Border control should have eyes like magnifying glasses, but lucky for me, they easily distracted when bored. I have nice hair then, and know how to paint my lips. To smile. Look helpless struggling with baby and another child. They rush to help.

I begin carry small amount drugs in cheeks, along tongue, between whistle of teeth. To speak was danger. Soon bosses demand I take more, and with Miguel in arms, and Juan hanging on skirts, both clutch teddies stuff with coke. No one prise teddy from children and pull off head.

Catalina

I'm lying on a towel, fastidiously laid over the bed sheet. Miguel smiles at that.

"The towel will be kicked aside, snagged on your rings, dissolved under our rusty wings. What's satin for, if not to crackle under us, to crisp and flame? We'll be worn to a sliver, the carpet will burn us, the table will bruise."

"Miguel, we can be each other's wound."

"I would rather grow in dirt, like a handful of seeds released and forgotten about. Obligations are a blight."

Our purple shadows hang from the wall, and we have a small space to discover much about humiliation and desire.

Today, Miguel dashes to my villa for sex; this is all he wants from me. He has never pretended otherwise.

The first time I met him I was walking my dog in the campo. He told me he was a surgeon, with a couple of hours to kill before he prepped for an operation. He told me his wife had died, but later admitted he has a partner and child. He's what my mother calls a 'snake oil merchant'.

A lot of people wouldn't understand how I became friends with Dee, while keeping my affair with Miguel hidden from her. From my point of view it was worth the anxiety and guilt of the deceit, in order for us to become best friends. There are few women as interesting as Dee, with such wide interests, funny, and kind. All the local Spanish women seem to care about is keeping their step clean, making their jars of olives, and pleasing their man with tortillas on the table. The other English women mostly seem to drink too much and worry about how to keep the wolf from the door.

With Dee I could talk about art and nature. When I took her to meet my parents on the island, she enjoyed these family meals, because her parents are separated and she never sees them. My parents only met Miguel on the day of the wedding. Whenever I tried to get him to the island he got furious.

"Do you think I can stand to try to be on my best behaviour for the whole trip? To pick up the right silver spoon or fork? To drink just the right amount and be witty? But not drink so much I become loud, and you have to kick my leg under the table."

"I wouldn't need to kick you, Miguel. Why do you have to exaggerate everything? My parents will say you're good-looking, and that'll be it. Come over next time I bring Dee over. We could have a party."

"You would love that, wouldn't you, Catalina? You're longing for Dee to discover I'm seeing you, because then I would have to choose between you."

"That's not it. I love Dee. I honestly think it would be fun for us to do things together."

"How about you coming to Mother's house then? You'd love it. She drinks out of the same glass she puts flowers in, and she doesn't have little scissors kept just for cutting the flower stems to the perfect angle, before arranging them daintily in a silver jug. She scrubs her plastic tablecloth so hard it's stuck to the table, and she eats off the same plates she uses to feed the dog. Come to my place, Catalina. I'm certain you would feel very comfortable at one of our family meals."

* * *

Dee finally discovers my affair with Miguel when she turns up unannounced at the villa. She walks straight in, and discovers us sprawled across the sofa.

Miguel doesn't miss a beat.

"Dee, what a nice surprise. I'm paying Catalina to give me a massage."

"Well, Miguel, that's a totally normal thing for you to do. Go ahead, don't mind me watching."

I try to improvise something like a sports massage. I feel awkward, and when I rapidly end it, Dee says, "Pay the lady, Miguel."

Tila

Because I'm too drunk to get home, I spend the night sleeping rough in the street alongside a car. When I wake up, I'm cold and stiff, so I walk about to work it off. I come across a woman I like the look of. More accurately, I stumble into her because I'm still drunk. I think she is homeless, and I have woken her rudely, so expect her to launch into angry-speak, but she accepts my apology graciously. She is not homeless, but she's preparing tracts to display on the streets, her bare feet on top of her sandals, nails painted red. She has long black hair, kohl around her eyes, and red lipstick. Sexy, middle-aged woman.

She shakes my hand, and introduces herself as Jill. She has a big suitcase, overflowing with papers, and tells me she lives in a tiny house, the size of a bus shelter. She jokes about me living in the house with her; says I can, because her ex-partner has their children, but she keeps a spare room for when she manages to get them back.

"It's the size of a shoe box. I wonder if it would be too small."

She shows me things she has found in newspapers, pamphlets, and wrappers, chucked on the street. She shows me poems and short stories she has written, inspired by garbage, which she then sticks up on bus shelters, or makes photocopies of to paste onto walls. I'm excited to realise I found one of her hammered-up poems once, and tell Jill it saved my life.

She doesn't laugh when I admit I dance in the streets, and says that when her children were small she could hold them in her arms and dance with them, too. It's lonely without them.

We go back to her house and on the way she starts talking about how she would like to poke down these houses, which are practically derelict.

I say "Do you mean literally poke them down?"

She says "Yes."

She points to one she'll poke down, next to a women's hairdressers.

"They'll put up a wall of bricks when I poke it down."

I say "Well let's do it," and start sticking out my tits and swaggering around.

She says "I know why I like you so much – all this aggression." She puts her arm around me.

* * *

Jill's tiny house looks like it's covered in clocks, the ones I once used in my art, dug up from an old robbery haul, all battered and old and gorgeous. When we get closer though, I see flattened tins cover it, not clocks.

She rushes around, grabbing food, apples, and bananas in hand. She gets us some dusty chocolate pudding in four thin slices then serves up massive pieces of a raisin pudding. A cat leaps up and starts licking the pudding left in the pot, and Jill says, "I should scoop out the licked bit," but then she decides to throw away the whole thing, and gets out a basket full of different flavours of cat food.

"Jill, I can't eat the pudding because I'm vegan," which isn't true.

"I can't accept that as an excuse."

Why can't I eat a thing when I'm lusting after women? I remember falling apart whenever Rita was in the room. One time she was a few feet away and I tried to eat a jacket potato with grated cheese but my hand started shaking so much I missed and it ended up in my lap. What if that happened now? That will happen. I'm tempted to tell Jill I hate food, that it started with school dinners and hiding meat in my pocket, feeding it to my dog under the table.

I fantasise that Jill and I are kissing, starting to remove our clothes, her saying I'm sexy, me taking off more clothes. She tells me I mustn't leave. I have no intention of leaving. She reminds me of a figurehead on a ship, and I imagine her battling the storm, leading everyone to safety, and being worshipped by them.

* * *

I meet Jill for a drink at *Waxy McFaggots*, where there are speakers in every nook. We settle in the sofa room, but an inexperienced and maudlin band takes the stage, and they are too awful to listen to, and impossible to talk over. Everyone leaves in droves, including us.

We sit outside a bar and, apart from the persistence of street beggars, are undisturbed, relaxed, and get quite drunk.

"Tila, your dancing is your way of expressing yourself. I wonder if you would like to audition for the performance company I direct? There's an open call next month. You should give it a try."

She hands me a flyer.

Fallout Studios

Fallout Studios houses a fluctuating collective of artists and performers who inhabit individual and shared studio spaces, rehearsal and performance areas. There's an opportunity for artists/performers to rent spaces when they become available and to audition for Fallout Company which performs nationally and internationally.

"You'll be put through your paces, but you don't need to prepare anything. You have nothing to lose by trying, and a lot to gain."

* * *

The journey to *Fallout Studios* turns out to be more complicated than I expected, and when I finally get there, the audition's almost over, but I wonder if Jill will let me have a go. She has moved on to asking everyone questions. She asks a girl "The first time you saw your girlfriend kissing another girl, who was it?"

She asks a guy "If a girl you fancy has just slept with someone else, and then comes on to you, would you, or would you not, sleep with her at that point – because of the possibility of encountering another guy's spunk?"

Jill gives me a chance to audition, and gets me to improvise. I'm put through quite an ordeal by this guy, Skinny, which lasts ages, and then I have to construct something using the skin of sour figs, and I end up eating them.

Jill asks me to stay after the audition and plays back the audition video. I'm really going for it, running round and I don't recognise myself at first because my jacket, my newest velvet one, makes me look quite cool.

"See how the camera likes you in close-up. Think of eating sour fruit as punishment for being late for an audition. It's not acceptable. Your work's very good, though. Get here on Saturday at ten."

As I'm leaving, I bump into Aaron coming out of one of the rehearsal rooms. It's only a couple of years since I finally got over my schoolgirl crush on him. As kids, we spent countless evenings burning treacle toffee at my house or his, while he kept assuring me that my mum would come back from her night out. Eventually mum's feet would be back in those slippers that always seemed to be empty on the living room floor.

As soon as mum went out, I would drag my bike from the garden shed and cycle round to Aaron's. One time I pulled off my jacket, and Aaron saw something poking out of my pocket. He said 'You're carrying round a Valentine's Day card,' and I said, 'Yes, it's from some guy'.

It was from my dad.

Sometimes, through the window, I still think I can see dad, leaning against the fridge, but he isn't actually there. It's just magnets holding drawings, some of them by me, but mostly done by dad.

I imagine how different my life would be if he had changed his mind about leaving, put his zip bag back on the side table, set up his drawing board and designed another plane, or even those two tiny boomerang things, just bits of a plane which earned him so much money.

"Tila, last time I saw you was the day you knocked over your desk and walked out of school, and no one could stop you."

"Aaron, don't you remember? We went shoplifting, and when we got caught your mum collected you straight away, but I had to wait at the police station for mum to pick me up after work."

"I do. And you were taken out of school, and had to see educational psychologists. Mum wouldn't let me near you again. Everyone thought you had gone to some dance school."

"Aaron, it's so good to see you, and the weirdest thing is, I dreamt about you recently. You were going to this market to buy wigs."

He says "That's freaky. I just walked in on my flat mate, who has long auburn hair, and she was completely bald. Turns out she wears wigs."

We go to *Marine Ices*, where you can choose one of fifteen flavours of ice cream, and I do the thing where I bend the spoon with my mind. Aaron loves all that.

"Remember the time we had a séance at my house and lifted a huge dining room table with our finger tips? We terrified ourselves so much we had to sleep in mum's room. We thought we could keep death away with a hanky soaked in perfume."

Aaron's licking the spoon, and talking about needing a boyfriend, and I realise we probably knew we were gay even when I had a crush on him.

We go over to his flat and he makes coffee.

"I just got back from Madrid. I was setting up a big deal."

I'm in disbelief that he made it without some sort of escort. Ever since I've known him he's always got so stoned he could barely find his way home.

"I ran my car through the doorway of a train at the crossing. I thought I was going into a tunnel or something. Do you still see your psychiatrist, because I really need one?"

I hate it when someone starts carelessly talking about my mental health, and Aaron's drug habit making him paranoid hardly compares with that. I'm sick of psychiatrists assuming I smoke weed and use cocaine and that my hallucinations are drug psychosis. I know plenty of drug casualties, but I'm not one.

I'm a spooky woman – reading minds and having out-of-body experiences. If I hadn't always been asking my mum, 'Am I real?' and having premonitions, and terrible dreams when I was a kid, my mum would've liked me more. I've read books about premonitions, and tried to understand, but people are the frustration, cunning and tricky, so you can never know or understand them. The mind reading happens still, but mostly I'm able to shut up about it, even when I know someone's telling me a full-on lie.

Only when I dance does everything make sense; the ideas flow through me and I paint with my body on the canvas of earth and sky. I practise for hours at a time. Here's how it is. With no more than a paper bag I can fly, hang, and hover. When I was eleven my paper bag got wet when Aaron opened a *Coke* can near it. I went ballistic because I hadn't yet realised I could fly without it.

Aaron asked "Do you seriously believe you can pluck everyone off the ground, between your finger and thumb?"

"Not everyone. That guy outside *Subway*, people have made him small."

"The shouty guy? Anyway, does it matter if he's tiny?"

"It matters if I want to talk to him. It would matter then, wouldn't it?"

* * *

Last night I dreamt I was supposed to go and get a potato so the schoolmaster could make crisps. I think I offered because I had already eaten the ones they had. He told me to get it on GM, which meant on credit, and I was trying to work out which shop would have potatoes. I passed a kid hiding out in the grass. I remember the shop I went into had bars of *Dove* soap. I woke up, calling out, 'Purlanchos'.

* * *

I'm buying books, which I know have been altered in some way by the people selling them – the endings are different. A lot of the bookshelves are quite empty and I feel strangely unsatisfied.

The book seller is killing huge yellow moths. At first he's just trying to catch them – they're flying against the lights – but he ends up really viciously killing them, squishing them. They keep forming into different groups and some try to escape individually. He says they have to be killed because they would breed and eat all the books and everything. There's a TV switched on in the room and they're batting into that, too.

It's pointless buying more books, because I can't escape into one, can't hold the last sentence in my mind long enough to join it to the next.

* * *

Mostly I pace the flat, my creativity consumed by medication. I'm sick of these drugs. No one should be this empty. I run a hot bath and dissolve the tablets one by one, pushing them from their plastic blisters into the water, where they make cloudy little currents, before sinking, semi-dissolved, to the bottom.

I climb into the water, and as I plough it I come across huge guns, beautiful ones – all different in design. A rifle's made of sculpted unusual wooden parts and metal. I keep finding more and decide to keep them hidden. The guns mean I can join a gang; everyone will want me to join theirs. I could probably run with several and will have women throwing themselves at me. Maybe I'll keep the women and not bother with the gangs. Someone rings and I ask how much the guns are worth; £650 each.

I pretend I'm somewhere completely different.

Heena

I crave the sugared almond days, the butter-cream sentiment of other people's lives.

I'm on the coldest step holding, against Catalina's thumping cries, a bag of goldfish. Suspended twists of tail and fin – my ocean breathing calm. I catch rainwater in a pan, pour it into my fish tank, filling it with freedom and light.

Last night was a vigil, watching as a dead fish slowly rose towards float, watching the movement of death enter its spine. Fish can be frozen in lakes and thaw out. Fish have been flushed away and then seen swimming round the toilet bowl. There's the thinnest of lines between coma and death.

Dettol smells of death. When I was small, I woke to an empty house, wandered into the garden and saw the mattress under my tree soaked in blood. I thought someone had been murdered and raced off on my bike to the bar. When I found Dad he told me my dog had been attacked and was lying in the shed. I brought him into the kitchen and put antiseptic on him, but when he shook himself, blood spattered everywhere, so Dad put him back in the shed. I went there to suffer with him.

While I was sleeping, Dad put my dog down. I would've done anything to save him.

When Mum left home, Dad insisted I go to live with Catalina and their baby at her villa. Recently, Catalina's eyes are glazed towards the banal. She won't pull herself out of it – it's an affliction causing her to see the green sign of the supermercado instead of the green of the ocean. She's happiest baking manic muffins, using up three pounds of almonds, chopped and whipped into shape, and blobbed into the tin tray circles.

"Catalina, what have you to look forward to? You're more under Dad's thumb than Mum was."

"Heena, try to be pleasant. You can't get on with anyone."

"At least I'm not interfering with anyone else's happiness. You come barging in and ruin everyone's lives. You don't like that you can't drag me around like you can with Sergio."

"Heena, I know we're miles apart, but let's try to get along for your dad's sake, for Sergio's."

"What exactly do you imagine I owe dad?"

Catalina gets weirder all the time, letting in complete strangers and rabbiting on to them about veganism. I say her hair has really grown, to compliment her, say it makes her much prettier, but really I don't like the way it grows. There is something freakish about it.

Today she's crying because the cistern cupboard is overheating, and she's convinced smoke's coming up between the sheets, though we have tried to assure her it's just steam.

* * *

It's Sergio's birthday party, and Dad insists I go. I'm making a mask to hide behind and stick on white hair, like a doll, and paint-on purple and green dye. I don't have much time as I left it a bit late to get enthusiastic. The masking tape runs out when I've used a couple of strips, so there isn't enough to stick head to neck.

Catalina asks me to get together a dish of wraps and tacos for twelve people. "Make sure there are some vegan ones, just salad."

They aren't actually vegan, because I sneak in mayonnaise. Catalina's such a hypocrite, cooking slabs of meat for Dad, and then insisting on animal rights. She has suddenly decided eggs have feelings, and is promoting an 'Egg Liberation Society', educating people and alerting them to this horror: that the egg and nest have but a few radiant hours together before they're cruelly separated by a massive clutching hand. Meanwhile, mother hen's revolving on a spit in the kitchen and has to listen as her offspring are remorselessly beaten, fried, or scrambled. I say maybe she could expend her energy and passion on ending nuclear threat or something. As she walks away I hear her spit, 'Murderess!'

I eat only brandy snaps, which are completely delicious, and I wonder how ginger could linger somewhere in my cells, how eating the biscuits could've awoken my five-year-old self stealing brandy snaps from mum's hidden supply.

On the sofa, someone opens a bottle of beer that explodes foam all over me. I pour a bottle that exactly fills the glass, but worry about the calories, and take champagne instead. Catalina decides she'll have some, too. I see Dad watching, and I jump away from her, because Dad would be glad if we were getting on. I stand on a chair and watch the last streaks of sunset through the window.

* * *

I wake at 3.45 am, drenched in sweat from a nightmare:

I have infuriated Catalina for some reason and her friends are all freaking out about what she'll do. She grabs a can of gasoline and pours it all over me and is trying to set me on fire. There's a huge chase with me trying to pull my clothes off while avoiding a lighter. I pass someone smoking, and manage to get away, because her friends are heading her off. But some dumb girl flicks a lighter and my right hand is on fire. I'm freaking out with the pain, and think I'm going to completely ignite. I manage to douse the flames and throw all my clothes right out of the window. I have a burnt hand and

Catalina's still crazed. Then comes a very sexy part of the dream, where a girl who's singing suddenly becomes the size of a spider and runs up me and all over me. I respond by getting down on my hands and knees and start chasing after her.

* * *

Catalina buys picnic things, and drags me and Sergio to the beach. Rice cakes banging on her arse sound like horses clopping and I turn around to watch them. Strawberry stained cashew nuts are produced. I'm a lapsed vegan, (Catalina calls me post-vegan), and I need not obsess over whether this is an egg glaze on the best bread.

I'm wearing dark sunglasses in the aching sun, but Catalina shows me how much better her green ones are. I try them on and they really work.

My dog, Nonny, takes off and I run around the beach saying, "I have money, a reward, for his safe return."

I catch sight of him and I run in the opposite direction, circling to try to meet him. I fail to catch him, but he turns up after two hours. Nonny drags me by a strange route, over the sand hills and we meet several dogs, one of them an Irish wolfhound, the tallest breed, and I worry how it'll react to Nonny, but it doesn't bother him.

I sit on an old green tarpaulin, left behind when some lorry shed its load maybe, and Nonny starts drinking from where it dipped and filled with water. I wonder if it's okay for him to do that. It can't be very clean. Then he jumps in and swims so sweetly towards me, and I help him out.

A dog sinks its teeth into Nonny's head and won't let go. The owner's being completely useless, and I yell for him to drag his dog off because when I pull Nonny away his dog follows with its teeth clamped into his head. He finally prises his dog off, but Nonny can't stand and is all floppy and unresponsive. We have to drive him to the vet.

This is as good as our family life gets.

* * *

When we get home, I bring the flat rocks I've collected into the house and Catalina complains that dust is coming off them and it is damaging her furniture. She asks why I brought them in and I say, 'For sculptures'. I carry them to the back of the house. Catalina has a neighbour's little boy under her arm and he starts peeing gleefully on me as I try to undo the door to get outside.

* * *

I receive a postcard from my mother that tells me nothing about her life, or how grandma is, or mentions how she's missing me. It shows a cat washing its paw, and replies to a question I don't remember asking: I don't recall love.

You were always imaginative as a toddler, with your friends the three-legged, blue Dardies, living behind the skirting board. But many kids have similar pals.

When I first started to become unhappy living at Catalina's villa, I began a kind of slow suicide, because I didn't make efforts to take in food. I started to waste away. I had no interest in the survival of my body, and I escaped by living mostly in my head. I found a way of shutting down my body entirely in order to escape my situation. It's so easy to say 'I don't care' to the body's demands if you don't want to live. There are times – even now – when I want to escape into the small space of the *Evian* bottle, become a breath of air squeezed into the smallest of spaces.

Meatless.

Here's how I disposed of Catalina in my head: She got me a bike for Christmas. It was a shopper bike, with a basket front and back. I locked it to a lamppost two streets away, and it got stolen piece by piece. Neighbour's kids used to come rushing in after school to tell me. At first they were nervous, saying 'Someone's nicked your saddle'. But then they realised how happy it made me, and they'd be all excited when another bit was gone. It took ages before the last bit of frame finally disappeared. One day someone managed to get it free, and that was it.

Free of her.

Aaron

I'm supposed to be getting food with Tila, but get dragged into a procession against my will, enticed around the corner by a young dancing boy. When I reach the café, Tila's with Ashish, who has only just joined the company. I've never really spoken to him – he's much older than most of the dancers – and his predilection for wearing women's clothing has made me shy the couple of times we've rehearsed together.

Tila is paranoid about the procession, convinced the various groups marching are after me and wanting to attack me and Ashish, because of how we look and act. "Aaron, we all recognise homophobia when we see it."

"You're always convinced someone is going to pull a knife. I think we're all fine. Relax, Tila."

Ashish is beautiful, dressed in a leather skirt and heels. He doesn't say hello to me, but holds a pair of socks against my crotch and says, 'Hmm' doubtfully.

Tila seems irritated when Ashish announces, 'I shall eat only crisps. I renounce the salad'.

I'm folding salad leaves, when I notice a slug and throw them down. Ashish has his back to me and white stuff is leaking out of his bag.

When I tell him, he just says, "Is there a bathroom here?" But, without even glancing at his bag or walking towards the bathroom, launches straight into, "Tila, darling, it's fifteen years today since I ran away to London, and some copper took me back to his bed instead of directing me to *Centre Point*."

"A lot happened, didn't it?"

"Darling, I met Brian Eno in the park, played cricket with Lemmy from *Motorhead*, smoked weed with *Genesis* and *Wings*, hung out with Boy George, stopped a cab for Bob Geldof outside *Hard Rock Café*, chatted to Paula Yates at Camden Lock..."

I say "Wow, that's really something."

"No, no, that's nothing! The ultimate thrill: I watched Kate Bush's rehearsals at *Rainbow Theatre* and had a vegetarian meal with her afterwards. Everyone thought I was her sister."

"Wow, Ashish, that's really something."

"An incredible show, so many amazing costumes and dances. Kate wore a special head microphone, so it didn't stop her dancing while she sang. She gave me her *Kick Inside* album, my most treasured possession. She wrote, 'For lovely Ashish, stay happy, lots of love, Kate Bush.'"

* * *

A series of disasters cause the other residents to move out of my block, culminating in a fire in the adjacent flat, which guts it completely. A persistent creep arrives to bang on my door, attempting to score drugs at all hours of day and night. I stop paying my rent.

I accidentally lock my keys and luggage in the flat on my way to the train station at the start of our dance tour and have to kick in the door to get my rucksack. Nothing was taken while we were away, so it seems no one desires my stuff, and so there's no point fixing the door. However, when the Polish guys in the flat above get wasted and start arguing violently, one of them gets pushed down the stairs and lands against my flat door, rolls in, apologises, and staggers out again.

* * *

I nearly don't make it for tonight's performance. I search the flat for my jacket, but one of my visitors must have stolen it, and I'm furious. I need a phone number I don't have, and some druggy woman is hanging around outside and won't get off my case when I walk outside.

In the administration office I look at the running order and clean my teeth at the same time. I almost miss my cue, and have to swallow the foam as I follow the line. Horrible!

The audience are all sat at round tables and most of them are children. Only a dozen adults, standing at the back. Ashish says "They won't know how to get involved. We could put them on our laps." I think he is joking.

After the show, he comes over to join us at the bar table, and he hesitates, unsure of where to sit, I suppose. Then he says "I'm just deciding which pose to take." After he sits down, I'm a bit sick from drinking and nerves. A thin stream of wine lands on Ashish's shoes. We both pretend not to notice.

Later, he leans over suddenly to kiss me, and a shred of tobacco transfers itself from his mouth to mine. I love it.

Ashish is pretentious, but irresistible, always starting sentences with something like, 'When I was walking The Great Wall of China, I thought of a recipe for...' but says he can't apologise for the fact he has done so many things and led a hundred lives.

He rings my house and leaves stupid flirty messages on my answering machine, and flatters the hell out of me. He offers himself to me like a gift it would be churlish to refuse. I'm not usually so available, and I'm amazed he has the tools to crack my shell. He calls it pearl diving.

* * *

Some weekends Ashish collects me in his van, hands me a joint, and delivers the countryside to me. He has musician friends with a recording studio on a farm in Granada, living pretty much like hippies – permanently stoned because they're surrounded by acres of marijuana.

Filled With Ghosts

When Rosa, who owns the farm, got busted she pointed to the acres of marijuana and pronounced that it was for home use, and they can't touch you for that under Spanish law. "She's Baronesa Something, so I'm pretty sure she'll get away with it, even in that quantity."

It's strange how you get used to being accepted for your choices, for who you are, by your friends, and then you're suddenly made aware that you're living in a bit of a bubble. Away from the farm and *Fallout Studios*, Ashish and I frequently threaten people with our lifestyle.

Ashish says "Aaron, this is nothing. If you had been around in the early eighties you would've really known homophobia. The government shoving pamphlets through doors warning not to share a toothbrush, a razor, a cup even, with the gays, because we were all infected with the Gay Plague, AIDS."

Tila grabs my glass when I move it away from her as she goes to take a swig. "I'm not worried about catching anything from you, Aaron."

Ashish drawls "Tila, darling, I think he just didn't want you to knock back his booze!"

PART TWO

Her goose bumps bleed from a botched leg-shave. Her hands won't work and her shoes don't fit. She is this Saguaros, a beautiful cacti, which can be shot full of holes, carved upon, knocked over, and stepped on, and will still store life-giving water, grow wild, and repair itself over time.

Diana

I wake frequently in the night, with nightmares of loss and a sense of unreality:

I go into the garden and accidentally set fire to a tree and become a bit drunk from eating fruit that has become alcoholic. The phone rings, and out of the house next door come three ages of Heena. I say "I have a baby again," and I'm hugging them. Grandma and Granddad appear in a kind of Victorian costume. Mia's little boy, Jhalib, has a disease which means he'll become very weak and will have to be given vitamin injections, but still won't grow properly. He's so beautiful and I know he won't be when the disease kicks in, and he'll also exhibit strange behaviour. Heena has a wallet and is putting a little black tray and safety scissors in it, and we're all excited because they fit in there, and I'm saying it's a magic wallet which will hold everything. Then Jhalib starts manically cutting up everything and Heena wonders why he's destroying her materials. I want the kids to cross the road with us, but they're dashing across by themselves. I'm with Heena and we see a couple of them have dropped a big toy bird and something's coming towards them as I try to get to them. I'm going down a huge shell-shaped steep path, holding onto Heena. It's difficult. I see the kids are falling into the water, and when I get to the bottom of the shell I realise I still can't get to them because I'm surrounded by deep water.

I open my lids slowly under the covers. Monstrous thoughts cram my head with spiky fluff, and purple-stained reflections bounce through the skylight. Not a rose on the bush outside now, the creeper strangles everything in its path, and then gives up itself. The shrubs are dark and mottled, and have long ceased to matter. There's a light today, hot like tomato soup, fragile as a whisper of cloth. For a minute I have the strongest feeling of being in the security of my childhood bed, sense the direction it faced, and the smell of clean sheets.

Here, herbs hang in bunches from Pilar's rafters: lavender, mint, thyme, and sage. Though they're neither poisonous or threatening, they remind me it was my hands that took the wheel of a red *Volkswagen Beetle* while its previous occupants were treated like the remains of a picnic, left for the wolves.

In the polar bear dawn, no luxury of routine staples my separate parts, they knock against each other, undisciplined. My escape tunnels are sealed, escape hatches blocked. I dimly recall a drill: use your pen as a sword, to cut through the heavy pall. Half-awake, I try to write on my pad, though when I wake fully my words have been obliterated by something, which had crept from the covers.

I'm treading a thin line between dispute and endeavour – knowing I might still be drowning – and the shore isn't safety. The prospect of victory is sandwiched between histrionic outbursts. From the point of view of lying in the gutter, I want to resist being hammered into life, and imagine never touching another human being again. I see the fork in the path, but can't choose.

The dangerous possibility of being found out means keeping a safe distance from as many people as possible, for their sake as well as my own. I'm afraid I'll blurt something out when I'm angry or upset. I can't believe I did what Miguel asked, out of shock and fear of the consequences, so at best I'm a coward.

It's unsurprising that I'm filled with self-loathing.

I see the murders in hallucinatory detail, see them reenacted over and over again in nightmares. I watch blood drip close-up, microscopically detailed, the structure of the corpuscles, a spider's web created over cloth fibre, composed, following the threads, spreading out fibre by fibre, slowly like an animal crawling along a blade of grass. The spider of blood is spinning, the mouths and teeth are open and tongues loosened, as veins spit. Then Miguel, holding the flawed amber glass, cheap and red-tipped, hollow, transparent, spilling into his open mouth, gurgling laughter, positively gleeful, like he just received the best Christmas present a child could ever have. Miguel, the puppet, jerky, fast. The blade naked for a brief interlude before he pushes it into flesh.

I walk into the kitchen and Pilar is at the sink peeling potatoes. She turns her head and shoulders, but stays aligned to an invisible force. She looks over my shoulder, so I look round to see who's there. No one, which is disconcerting.

She sits me at the table, and starts tapping her hand the way the very old do, marking the time they have left, making a statement out of it. She rolls an imaginary something, bread perhaps, between fingers and thumb. But she isn't that old, and she isn't absent, she's astute – sharp even.

Pilar says "Over time, body grow beyond pleasure and stiffen in subtlest ways. Mind stiffen too if you don't keep it loose."

This is how I look forwards: I tinker with my mind. I take everything apart, dropping my memories into a sink of brackish water, poking them down the plughole until they disappear into disturbance and rot. There's no other way to survive weeks that are already shaped and lie in front of me, ready to be stepped into. Art's my escape.

I sit at Pilar's kitchen table doing tiny paintings, instigated by a dream I had:

A girl with long hair is painting an egg series: an egg

in leopard print; an egg in big boots; one in bondage gear. An egg arrives at the kitchen window and knocks, another lies back in the dentist's chair. Eggs play the piano: swim in a fish tank; eat humans for breakfast; roll them down hills after boiling them in onion skins for decoration.

Whenever I paint, I'm where I began, the enjoyment of colour and shape in space. I feel the old sureness and confidence as I put one fragment against another. You can't be a visitor when you paint. You have to get under the skin to the messy, bloody heart of the thing.

This one shows a white-gloved hand snatch an egg from the nest, as a chain of little arms reach up to rescue him. Eggs scuttle under magicians' cups, fry themselves on the bonnet of a broken-down truck in the desert showing the future in their yolk, and throw themselves at bastard MPs. It's a relief to do these small, odd, figurative paintings, they say something tiny yet important.

I have a weird fondness for eggs. My first week at school, we were asked to take an eggshell to school. Dad showed me how to put a pinprick at each end and blow the contents into a saucer. My cheeks hurt from blowing, but it was worth it because the hollow egg was so beautiful and perfect. I wrapped it in cotton wool, and got it to school without spoiling it. The teacher told us we were going to grow cress in our eggshells, and she dug in her nails and pulled it apart.

After all the years of wanting a studio, and Miguel refusing me, I've found a space. The rent's cheap, and though I hate to take more money from Pilar, who does so much for me, she brushes my protests aside.

"Soon you sell. Everyone want your work. You make us rich, girl."

In the dusty cavern of my space at *Fallout Studios* I'm creating an installation using garments, with descriptions on the back like 'thin neck', 'broad shoulders', etc. Well, it will end up being so much more, the details are still a bit elusive. I see a Kate Bush cushion, her face and 'WAKE UP' printed on it. I want to build up a suspenseful atmosphere, like trying to prevent stacked shelves from smashing down and spilling their contents everywhere.

I'm also embedding stained glass fragments in a doll. I've been making some very intricate sculptures out of reclaimed materials, mostly found in skips. I use an engraving point to make holes; such complicated designs which involve all kinds of materials, including *Roses* chocolate wrappers and lots of glittery gold, which I'm sewing on as costumes. While I'm making the figures, I bend back a doll's head too far and it snaps off. Jill gives me some nails, the heads of them square and covered with red material. I fix the settings for all the figures because I realise they're too weak, so I'm putting in more nails and making them strong and beautiful. I intended to place the scenarios on plinths, but Jill suggests I fix them to the gallery wall, and I think that would work. I think bread will be involved in the final installation.

I'm plaster-casting from a doll, outside in the sunshine – I have so little time to produce them – to make all the heads and limbs, and paint tights on the legs – that I realise I'll have to buy a load of cheap plastic dolls and customise those instead. A string of objects get caught in the hedge, and everyone's trying to help. I'm cutting thick wedges of napkins with Jill's material scissors and denying I'm using them.

I'm overwhelmed when I find myself an art agent. Jan Morel knows so many important critics and buyers, and can give me the best advice on what will sell. After so many years restricting myself to Pilar's kitchen table, squashed into a corner while she chopped the tomatoes for gazpacho, I pour my soul into all kinds of work. It had never occurred to me to work outdoors, or that any material can become art if the idea's strong. Being around other artists, surrounded by their ideas, has totally opened my eyes to possibility.

Miguel used to say, "Nobody's stopping you doing what the hell you like. You just make excuses for yourself."

In many ways that was true, but I felt held back by him, his drinking and drug taking, and escaped into the tiniest of *Biro* scribbles. Jan has expert judgement, but it doesn't stop me from suffering exhibition-related anxiety. I can't even find a sharp craft knife. The other artists are pre-occupied, but I find someone has been sellotaping craft knives under all the surfaces in the studio.

* * *

Certain people will have to show up before I can say tonight's a success. Jan tries to keep me calm but I have to introduce gallery owners and reviewers to the show, and I'm very aware of how smart they look in blazers and scarves. I feel very inferiorly dressed and presented.

All the exhibits are being photographed, one by one, in the gallery. Entering, I see dirty footprints on the doormat, and know I'll leave my own all over the gallery carpet, so I scrub my feet over and over until they're clean and I can go in.

Mia looks amazing in a blue Japanese kimono. She's talking about her 'just before the change' baby, and how she had to engineer it to happen. I pretend I don't think she left it far too late. She gets too close to someone waving a fag around and her kimono's badly burnt, so she starts wailing about life and how terrible it is, how it changes in such a short time from everything wonderful to something terrible.

Later I fall into a drunken heap with a couple of friends, but other friends rush me down the corridor to explore the rest of the exhibition.

Aaron, looking very young and gorgeous, arrives and I want to show him off. I show him the tiny beautiful pictures and sculptures I've made out of natural objects – they're far from the big industrial urban sculptures that everyone else seems to be making.

My daughter, Heena, finally turns up, declares her love for Francisco, and drives me mad. I'm furious he has given Heena his phone number, because I know she'll be calling him all the time. He puts Heena on his shoulders and pretends to finger her as he walks past me. Then he tastes his finger and announces, "Mmm, she tastes like her mother."

At times like these I long for a studio of my own, away from these performers, who think everything revolves around them and their act.

Some of the artistes go off early, and Jan is furious and asks for them to be brought back. Heena's kissing Francisco, which angers me, but I realise he's only a couple of years older than her, still a kid himself, so what's the point of trying to intervene? Heena will go further the more I push her.

"None of your business, Mum. Like you care."

Miguel

For my father, killing was a release from a kind of frustrated vitality – irresistible, always the same and yet also different. He told me sparrows, linnets, thrushes, all demand a spray of pellets through them. In my village their bodies are always worn around the waist on a string, like a belt. Father said the origin of the smile was amongst apes, who bare their teeth in mockery at the weak or unstable in the group. It's a matter of culling the weakest in the troop. To be alive, is no more than to be in the moment before it ends.

When my father showed me how to kill a goat, I was horrified. I was six years old. I watched him slit the throat, and it became my job after that. It was how to be a man.

My father was old then, but still fighting – he was always fighting. When he was captured in the war, imprisoned and sentenced to death, I bet he still wore the medals on his chest, still shined the buckles on his belt and boots. A gentleman soldier.

Catalina asks me "Which war was it?"

"Maybe all of them. Mother says he cut open a horse to climb inside for warmth."

"Siberia, then?"

"Maybe that's an exaggeration. When I wear his furry cap I think of Russia and vodka."

"Miguel, face the facts, war exposed the error of his ways without providing any answers. It provided the excuse to drug it all away."

"Oh, let all the visions rain down. They hurt less than pebbles."

Filled With Ghosts

Diana doesn't want me anymore. She didn't have my father to explain things to her. Is there a way of getting rid of someone without drama, as easy as slipping away under water?

Should I have knocked out their teeth so there wouldn't be dental records? Death's a small matter. I would happily endure the boat journey, plugging any leaks with my hair.

Living with Catalina used to be easy, her thinking I can mend everything, save her from the pain of being alone in her villa. But strings hold me back, the big red tie of my wedding outfit. The gift boxes and wrapping paper are now crushed, but my wheels are suspended, and still spinning.

The marriage took place at Catalina's parents' house, on the island they practically own. I travelled by boat – I would never get in a plane. As the boat landed, we were saluted by a giant foot, three hidden humps of giant toes. Everything there is built to breathe in circle, with a circular horizon, so there can be no other kind of architecture than circular.

Catalina says "There's no such thing as eternity, but at least the giant toes last as long as we can imagine. They're chipped into poetry. Stone's dead, but everlasting at the same time."

I say "In the house of the dead, the sun has gone down a billion times, so it tricks you into understanding eternity. This is real progress, evolving through sandstone rock."

The wind's strong on the beach. It blows over the lichen and makes a whistle of the grass. It's a happy sound. We walk along a path whose score of mossy bog sucks at our boots. Whenever I feel nailed in, writhing inside a body that doesn't fit, I like to escape the crowds, and enter rock pools to feel the nibble of fish. At times something seasonal, periodic, stops me wanting to engage with anybody.

* * *

I'm always trying to butch Sergio up, because Catalina encourages him to behave like a girl, shuffling around in her satin pointy shoes. It makes me feel physically sick. My father once beat me for putting on my mother's hat. He said you nip it in the bud, otherwise you'll wake up one day, a grown man, and want to wear women's clothes.

Catalina says "Sergio's only a baby," and lets him hide under a long fringe, because going to the barbers is such a hateful ritual.

My daughter, Heena, is less of a problem and now more useful. She spends days drawing intricate labels to stick on the small bottles of olive oil and herbs we sell. We make more money on the island than anywhere else because there are a large number of ex-pats and congregating hippies there. They love acupuncturists and herbalists – they're into yoga and alternative lifestyles and soft drugs.

* * *

Catalina isn't afraid of blood. She's not squeamish when I talk about stepping off the boat and finding yourself in a shark's stomach. What sweet suicide, and what a journey, to feel yourself as muscled as tongue, invincible like a second row of teeth. I order snapper in the restaurant, and Catalina doesn't know where the meat is, or how to extract it.

"It seems all jaw and skeleton, a very distant cousin to the fish I cook at home."

She takes the skeleton home for her collection. Snapper and vodka make a beautiful, cold, brutal combination. Chill and clean. I love the accusing angle of the jaw.

Catalina sees me open my breast as a sanctuary for sinner. She see them beating on the door, and I answer their prayers, and accept payment for giving them

45

redemption. What satisfaction would she gain if I cast myself back in the water? I would cross to the other place, where sharp sand provides a hiding place for strangers who come with darkness.

If she thinks she can escape, she's wrong. I'll hunt her down. Catalina thinks she's so strong, and can fight me every way, but when I tell her I've killed before, now she's suddenly afraid!

I take my knife and suck the blade. Look, I'm hanging out red streamers, releasing the kite of my belief, flooding everything in a rush.

Why would she leave?

I've done nothing wrong.

* * *

I'm surprised how glacial the temperature runs in this blue-veined landscape, like limbs whose track marks tell their own story. Dispersed, I integrate myself into brick dust and paint myself into the distemper of walls. My eyes lose their thick film and become transparent blue – all-seeing. There's a strip of runway on either side, lantern lit, and a roofless palace, ruined, abandoned. When I pull open the door I see limbless creatures, pulling themselves across the floor.

There's no salvation, just the lair of mistaken beasts. Purple light strains through a crack in the wall, and I climb through towards a sumptuous feast laid out. All fruit, many I don't recognise. I wonder if I'm the only guest, or if I'm even invited. A faint murmuring fills the space and I feel a shimmer echo in my bones. I touch a piece of fruit and it collapses, hollow, eaten from within. This is my table of discarded desire; a mocking display.

I always lead my women along a gravelly path towards houses whose crackly yellow windows are like greaseproof paper wrapped around loaves. Treacle toffee and toffee apples convince them this is a carnival and if they cross my palm with silver I'll tell their fortune. I reveal that their future only mirrors and diminishes their past, that in age they'll forget who they are and why. With no more sap in them, they'll snap when they try to bend in the wind.

Pilar

When Dee finally have enough of Miguel, Dee carry on stay with me, because truth is she never have another home. Her parents separate, and when she fall in love with Miguel, she also fall in love with safe house, because I more like mother to her.

When I ask how she feel now she push out Miguel, she get teary, and I don't want twist knife in wound. Their business is their business. Dee welcome stay here as long as she like. Miguel take Heena live with him and Catalina at villa and Heena furious about this, say Dee not care about her, send her live with stranger. Heena at difficult age, and maybe that why Dee let her go? Miguel lucky to find a rich girl to fall in love with him. I don't think he good catch.

Best for me now, Miguel not lurking around house, judging everything I do. I give up crimplene skirts and dresses for tracksuit and trainers. I keep me on toes, like a panther, ready to pounce. I not need wear handbag on wrist from time I get up and peel heap of potatoes until I go to bed, for fear Miguel rob me blind.

Sure, I not perfect either, I thieve, but women my age invisible, and if they search me I play menopause card. Anyone ask what I have in pockets, I tell them mind their own fucking business. Should be glad I not nick whole case of wine, and not pull my knife on them.

Catalina

I lie awake tonight after closing the shutters behind Miguel. When he leaves I continue to hold him in mind, knowing the danger surrounding him in this abject village, where people keep their pleasure tightly corked in bottles. I'm certain he's going to see Diana, but he also carries his camera, and will be looking for warm hearts and the opportunity to take souvenir pictures. He has a drawer stuffed with drawings and photos of all the women he has stripped naked. I deal with it, and only under the provocation of alcohol does my amazing mask sometimes slip.

I compete with Dee.

Miguel and I don't go out in public together. When we get hungry we listen to our musical stomachs, and the nearest we get to a social life together is dancing in evening clothes in my bedroom. He slowly takes off his tie, a small gesture which I exaggerate, ripping off my clothes; the salmon silks, the French knickers with small pearl buttons, so loose they're hanging from my hips. I wear my camisole with tiny carved egg buttons and my hair falls as rich as any lion's and as dark as my thick bush. Later, there'll be grey hairs amongst it, and it'll get sparser. I've seen that on older women with my own eyes.

A fly lands on me, takes off, and lands again.

When I life-model for Miguel, he sometimes draws me respectfully small within the architecture of my room, but at other times he climbs a stepladder and draws inches from me, in massive close-up. He draws my ribs so big, uncovered by flesh, and the deep, deep hollow leading down to my tiny flat belly button.

Miguel also draws deer, an apricot, a tarantula;

things that have touched him in ways he has been unable to express in words. Or he photographs them.

He collects playing cards too, often muddy and mangled, which belong in the trash. He scribbles the date he finds them, in black marker pen, over the hearts and spades, diamonds and clubs. I pick up a card labelled September 10th 1994, and invent my own wishful diary.

I imagine:

We have cowboy hats and two horses tethered to a tree. We rub sharpened sticks together, striking a spark to make an open fire. Fireflies and a night spent around a camp fire with a pot of bubbling soup.

We listen to crickets and lonely howls, wear blankets with holes cut in the middle. No fences, no structures, stoking the fire, and keeping all those glowing eyes at a safe distance.

* * *

We're slumped on concrete steps, where rivulets of piss – or worse – fill the cracks and race in dust-inspired mayhem towards the other side. I'm holding an angry pen. If I could write Miguel into a more manageable form it would defeat the object of him, but I can't be around his drama and self-obsession any more. He no longer entertains or engages me.

I won't back down this time; I'm shaving our relationship down to the bone. He's perched now, baggy-beaked like a pelican, ready to scoop me up as soon as I start to walk away.

"Cat, you always blow everything out of proportion. You never get the right answers because you don't ask the right questions."

"Miguel, you promote fear like bubble gum or washing powder. Every home should have it. I measure out my life in dirty coffee cups, the slow drip of the coffee maker marking out my time. Your shaving scum accumulates around the sink like the diary of a species."

Miguel's stubbly before noon, and his afternoon face scratches me. We're flotsam and jetsam, tossed amongst the bones he collects and turns into sculptures. When he's drunk, he makes wooden ships from tree branches, and seals which he paints coal black and glossy. Stoned, a wasp inside a jar is all the entertainment he needs.

Is this how time's best spent?

Or, in the bedroom, thinking up ever more imaginative and dangerous ways of making our orgasms intensified?

Beige over belly isn't a good look. "Miguel, buckle up your man belt, and drag your tired imagination from the bar seat."

"You only want to humiliate me. You claim to have travelled beyond hostility and found an answer in silence, but still want to shape my thoughts with useless trinkets."

"Miguel, I remember when your eyes flashed with passion. Your drugs damaged them, dispersed your passion, and weakened you."

He throws walls around himself, guards himself from my path. Today he's tripping on mushrooms, strong in his refusal to travel further with me. I try to wrench him from the apathy of Sunday and force him into the tingle of a Saturday high.

I say "If I could unravel you, take hold of a thread and tug, perhaps I would find you at the centre."

He says "I drink a lot and eat pies; that's every reason for a belly and dull thoughts."

Miguel has a place within his mind, zipped up for the most part, like skin protects the mango; his place of darkness, where he cries out for the father he lost. His childhood held neither glitter nor tinsel. Clowns and cake were choked down to sink into black bile. I thought he was the real thing until my growing belly stopped us in our tracks; stopped me breathing in nicotine; had me sucking on *Solero* lollies instead of bottles of *Sol*.

Filled With Ghosts

Before she found out I was screwing Miguel, I would take Diana to her favourite spot on the island, a waterfall in the forest. She made paintings so realistic I could feel the pounding spray on my face as I inhaled the oil paint. Her arms were always covered in paint, whereas mine were covered in flour. I would laugh at her because she even burnt toast. "You scrape off the top layer of charcoal into the bin like it's in the recipe."

* * *

Today, Miguel has condescended to walk into the countryside with me, so we can pick blackberries. I've agreed to make him his favourite – apple and blackberry pie.

A speckled hen, immune or immortal, pecks in the grit at the side of the road, and makes me think we have a chance of escaping being flattened by ignorant traffic. A black cat crosses in front of us, traffic sees it off. A horse leads the way up the steep main road, until a motorbike tearing past spooks it. The horse's rider apologises to the traffic as it side-steps and shimmies in front of it.

When we take shelter in a barn, I listen to rain on a roof whose holes are papered over and sag with fraudulence. Miguel sags with the heaviness of knees and the purple of his hair runs into the corner of his mouth like a poisoned smile; honeysuckle stubble's tinged like his blackberry-stained overalls.

Miguel ate most of the blackberries as we picked them, and he pukes over his jacket. In the kitchen an acrid smoke hangs, because I've burnt the stewing apples, and made the smallest blackberry pie ever, sweetmeats from the blackness of time.

"The crumble was invented by a pastry fuck up, this we know. Sure, recipes are as complicated as any other theory."

When I go to serve it, Miguel can't even face the pie,

and he hurls the fish spatula with the accuracy of a knife-thrower, cutting me from nose to lip. He cuts my flesh to the bone, and yet I feel nothing. I see a dangerous red, a flood, a mist, or veil. I feel the temperature, hear the sound of the ocean depths in my ears. I taste iron, but also cinnamon sugar on my lips, which I've bitten in my fever. If I had taken the bread knife to the pie, instead of the fish slice, I would be dead. If crumbs stick, pick them up or draw around them. A crumb will grease the shape of things to come.

* * *

Enlightenment occurs when knowledge is suddenly seen through new lenses, changing the past as much as the present and future. I can't believe I gave Miguel so many chances. Why have I not challenged him? There's no need to fail each other any more. I'll find a way of leaving him.

For now, I say I'm going out for fags and just keep walking and hugging myself.

Tila

Jill's leading the session today, and I'm desperate to seduce her but, despite the ridiculous sexual tension I feel, I'm not sure she's interested. I offer to help her clear her room, because she's sorting through paintings into those she wants to show, and those she doesn't. Some are big, un-stretched canvases. She's discovering some interesting ones.

Sweaty work, so she offers me a bath. I'm so nervous and excited around her that I leave the taps running without putting in the plug, and the water drains away, using up gallons of water. Jill's really upset about wasting water, because it's so scarce, and says she'll share the bath with me. I find that exciting, then I realise she means I'll bathe first and then she'll get in after.

Dozing in the bath and half-awake I have an erotic dream:

I've taken off my shoes, so I'm walking barefoot. I have to pee. They're telling me how dangerous it is outside, so I'm peeing inside the tent, on the material of the floor, but then someone starts to come in to see what it is, so I quickly move outside onto the grass. I'm sneakily sexual with Diana while people are around, hidden by the tall grass. Later she lies down and says she hasn't given me a kiss all night, but I just give her a quick peck on the lips.

Whenever I'm with Jill I always feel a wave of desire, almost like a wave of loss, a wave goodbye, a wave that seems to be carrying her away from me somehow, even when she is beside me. She pulls me in opposite directions, but if I can just find that elastic moment in the middle, I feel I can dance forever, my skin goosebumped, like I am plucking the same feather over and over again.

We walk out of Jill's flat, tough-looking in our leather jackets and *Levis*, and we see a group of hippies coming the other way. Jill recognises Mia amongst them, clutching her bag, a big stuffed triangle with a design of an Indian face stamped on it, no handle.

Mia hands me her beautiful baby, and I see how everyone is with him. Jill says how worthwhile and totally absorbing being with your baby is. Mia hands me a jar of food and a spoon, and at first the little boy can't handle me feeding him the strange mushy food, but then he gets used to me. He beams, and it's heart breaking.

* * *

I go to watch a performance at *Fallout*, an experimental piece. I'm virtually without sight – my vision's blurred. I keep walking the wrong way all the time, back towards the exit, and I clutch my ticket, trying to find my seat. I sense Aaron's watching me, like I'm in a film, or am a ghostly presence.

I say aloud "We're doing this all wrong," in a Miss Piggy voice, because some of the performers are dressed like muppets. I'm told off for talking, and a girl whispers that the audience and stage are wired up for sound like at a museum, and if we talk loudly we'll set off the alarms.

Someone I don't know hands me a drink, and I start talking to her, and she has dust on her beard. When I look around, everyone's in circular rows and in 'gesture', covered with gold makeup, kind of like Tutankhamun's casket. They have it over their hair and faces and someone passes me a pot of very gloopy gold makeup. I realise everyone's waiting for me. I take my glasses off and start putting on the gloop, but find it really difficult to get to the back of my head. I wonder if I should ask someone to help me.

Aaron's really enjoying the show, but I can only see heads, and wonder if, like me, he's hearing about himself in the stories. At the end, a woman hands out invitations for the next one, and it says, 'Tila in centre again.' She tells me she isn't allowed to take part in the next one. They're handwritten.

As I'm given one, Aaron says, "I'm off to *Resort* to do a dance class. Coming?"

I realise I'm wearing roller skates and everyone else has trainers. Aaron suggests the swimming pool, but it's freezing cold and I'm totally reluctant to go in. Aaron dives in, but I can see there's a huge sea urchin on the bottom. I think of a clam and how it might trap my leg. I see a huge sea monster leaning down, and it's vicious because a chimp's controlling it. When I go outside, I see the whole church – like a metal building pulled up by a huge crane. Aaron's yelling because his hand's crushed when it flips onto its end, imprisoning him. I go around the corner and a huge tanker's being lifted, and the only way I can avoid being crushed is by grabbing onto it. It swings out over a huge drop and I keep hold, exactly timing when to leave go as it swings back over land so I'm not crushed. I feel calm and focused throughout – no panic – which is why I manage to survive.

Becca's leading a rehearsal of *The Fallout Group* today. It's supposed to be a creative jamming session involving various artists and performers, whoever wants to get involved. The seats are set out facing each other, and Becca starts teaching something involving playing cards which is really complicated and which I'm failing to grasp. I'm writing things down and want to work things out on my own for a bit, but we're put in groups of three. I'm scribbling stuff on to the cover of my passport. Not a fantastic idea.

After rehearsal we're sharing out some cake on a plate. Everyone cuts off a huge amount and leaves one girl with hardly anything and she's furious and flings the plate and the remaining scraps at the wall.

* * *

I go for a drink with Jill and when I only have three euros left, not enough to pay for my round, I stagger off to get cash. I've been drinking tequila, but when I get back I order pints. The barman is some hideous bloke with a bleeding head who says I've had enough. When I protest, he says I'm banned.

I try to have a serious conversation with Jill. I really want to impress her, but I can't settle on an idea. I hover round it, land and spin off again. I know my words should be the key to clarity, and I try to speak the truth, to say things that make sense at this moment in time.

I say "Age five, I was genuinely amazed when I got yelled at for writing my family's names on the bed sheet. I had also scratched their names into the varnish of my new bed."

Jill shows me her most recent piece, which she'll hammer onto a city wall: Bully.

She shivers in discord, joined to a bear of a man like spittle between the bully's teeth. In the reckless shape of new beginnings she shears herself, she shivers in discord. Her emerging skull fills with new decision like spittle between the bully's teeth. There's a world of hair surrounding her, a morbid compass, She shivers in discord. Isolated on the chair she's spread like spittle between the bully's teeth. She gathers the hair in a hessian bag and holds her being, She shivers in discord, like spittle between the bully's teeth.

I ask her "Do you believe men are always the bullies? Or is it only Spanish men?"

"Well, all men have the power, though in my experience, it's only while women don't have power they behave reasonably, like empathic beings. When they attain power, usually by behaving like men, they're corrupted by it as readily as men are. They become domineering and know it all."

"Does power over other human beings always lead to corruption?"

"Tila, I believe women would start wars too. I'm not one of those who believe there would suddenly be a reasonable and caring world, if it was ruled by women. Some women are shits, just as some men are."

"Well, I don't think the problem's about trying to make it in the world, it's about realising everyone has to make it over and over again."

* * *

I arrive late for the shoot. I miss buses, get myself lost in the parkland and can't find my way out. I walk for miles, increasingly lost. When I ring home I just get an answer machine. I eventually find some people pulled up on a path but they won't help me because they're hanging out there to eat and drink. I think I might never find my way out and know how worried Jill will be. It all looks familiar, but that's because I'm going round in circles in a vast expanse.

When I eventually find the shoot, there's an amazing house and famous people are arriving. It's a crowded outdoor set, I can't find Jill, and no one knows if she has arrived yet. I have a half-joking argument with a woman that ends up with her chasing me and trying to attack me with a big stick, and I find myself far away from the main stage, lost in the crowds.

I find Aaron with money piled up on the table in front of him to get the drinks in. I feel like someone's pulling a needle out from the inside of my throat.

Jill appears, heavily made-up, and in a leotard. She says "We're going to start with the Madrid Dance." I say I haven't rehearsed it so have no intention of doing it.

There's an audience of extras crammed all around a tiny stage, which is set up for spoken word with a microphone. A middle–aged guy with a wavery voice is compere and I think anyone could do a better job than he did. I'm disturbed by one line: "I can't find the suit he was murdered in," which I think refers to Aaron.

* * *

Some actress we expected has vanished from the list. There's a river and a baby gets pushed into it in her pram. There's more than one in the river. I see one being safely rescued on another shore, but someone says an Indian boy has drowned and because he's Indian no one seems to care. One of the children is trying on my boots. I'm glad to be amongst the children at the event, which is all about people winning prizes, like the *Oscars*.

* * *

I say I can't stay the night, but Jill's in her element and desperately wants to. She finds out Aaron is in a hotel room and asks if she can stay too, and Aaron says, "Yes we can get you a room for tomorrow," but she wants to stay that night. I wander to the bathroom and wash with someone's animal sponge. I can't find my way back to their room, which I remember has no number. Aaron gave me directions but it's a massive hotel. I come across Diana in her room and she says she wants to be alone, but she won't kick me out.

* * *

I'm walking through the parkland alone because Jill is adamant about staying and I want to find someone to give me a lift. My throat's still full of something like bubble gum and I can't speak or breathe properly. I'm pulling out a load of it to free my throat, but it's still blocked and I wonder if my tongue has fallen back into my throat. I see pointed hats and a life-size bottle of *Matey*. A sea of mind, and an island floating in it.

* * *

I realise I can't leave, and when I go back, they are shooting the part Aaron has been rehearsing. I sit down in the audience. It seems to be in German, and doesn't make sense for a while, but then I understand it. I remember Aaron showing me a newspaper article he based the piece on, about someone offering a place for a lady cat prepared to sniff out the mice there.

In a break, I go to look for Aaron and three police cars rush off. I can't find him and I think he's probably somewhere cool picking up Mexican food, or whatever. Finally I see him, alone, walking my way, and I take his hand. He seems enormously tall, and I feel immensely small.

The shoot continues until dawn, and I desperately need sunglasses, mine are scratched and letting in sunlight. After the shoot, we go back to the studio, where Jill prepares food. They're trying to get at least a two euro food contribution out of everyone, but I have nothing left and won't be getting any more till next week. I'm completely jealous Jill's talking to some woman, and I try to prevent them getting on by refusing to acknowledge anything the woman says. But Jill seems to be getting on so well with her.

The room is very crowded, with a lot of costumes on hangers, and we sit down on the big raffia mat with a blanket over it. I'm smoking and accidentally set fire to the raffia. I start beating it out and asking for water, but people won't believe it's on fire because I have my hand over it and a blanket to try to smother it. Then it gets worse. Someone passes me water and I chuck it onto the flames as people shift their stuff from the mat. I manage to put it out but everyone seems angry with me.

* * *

I destroy a huge blow-up male figure with a knife. Or rather, I cut into it in a dissecting way. I'm waiting for

Jill to come back to me. Time feels all washed out and stumpy. It's like waiting for blood to flow, then having only blackberry-stained fingers when I push them in. Is this the speed she was talking about? Just enough pressure to make the connection and know you're alive.

I keep getting confused with where I'm going. I'm describing where I live now to the bus driver, or is it an old address? I don't know how to describe where I want to go. So scary.

* * *

I end up breaking into Jill's house, smashing her kitchen window and barricading myself in her bedroom. Finally, I realise there's no point in staying any longer, she's not coming back, and I must leave. I pick up her address book from beside the telephone, and crawl down the street with Jill's pink pyjama bottoms falling down. I'm terrified.

* * *

A bus pulls in – it might be the right one. Everyone on the bus is staring at me and I find a number that I think I recognise, but the address book's turning into mini TVs when I try to read it. Someone walks up to me and starts talking, and I have to get off the bus before they harm someone.

* * *

Jill is still missing. There's a ceremonial meal and the blade comes off the knife and I try to get it back on without cutting my fingers. I have nothing to say to strangers. It might be five in the morning, or five at night, but time means nothing. Rather, this is the moment when dust settling on my thighs makes me ache at the sun.

Diana's a true friend, she would never turn me out like Jill has, nor find an Ashish like Aaron has, leaving me out of everything.

It's alright, I know the way to Diana's door.

Heena

Grandma takes me and Sergio, and her lager cans, to sit on *El Gato Bar* terrace, where there's a view of the whole of Granada. She can't afford to buy drinks here, but no one questions her arriving with a booze-filled plastic bag. Part of her satisfaction comes from being in the posh surroundings.

"Footballers drink here," she says, and relaxes with cans of beer she has nicked from the supermarket.

A yellow helicopter flies overhead, disturbing the autumn leaves in massive rustling eddies, whipping up wrappers on the ground. Helicopters are the most unlikely things to stay up in the air: erratic and untrustworthy, they never settle. The helicopter lands on a rooftop, only metres from us, bringing an injured passenger, and a badly-dressed loved one carrying a clumsy handbag. The red-blanketed figure on the trolley is pushed into the lift to be loaded onto the ambulance at street level.

Grandma is crossing herself and muttering her prayers. However lapsed a Catholic she may be, in times of terror she calls on God, and helicopters are high on the list of terrors. She says police helicopters are all-seeing.

Whenever dad returns, he pulls out the fuse to plunge the house into darkness, and no one can move around then for fear the books and newspapers piled up everywhere will come crashing down.

Grandma's a hoarder, not of rubbish thankfully. But nothing which was once useful can be chucked away. It makes her feel disloyal if it is.

Grandma and Dad put up with each other for a

while, and then he disappears for weeks, until he chooses to disrupt our lives again. At some point he turns up, bringing cakes home on the bus; dropping them in the aisle, or on the street. It's the saddest thing, him fucking up everything even when he tries to make things right.

Today is Sergio's birthday, and Grandma's putting the finishing touches to a cake heavily weighted with action figures. I try to carry the tray of glasses, but almost collapse, dizzy, onto my knees. I see a plastic triceratops skeleton has fallen into the pond and I wade in to get it, slipping on the mossy edge and ending up on my ass in slimy water. Someone laughs and asks if it's wet out, and I realise I can't leave and go home.

This is my life.

The doorbell rings and it's Dad arriving with an entire party, food, and presents for Sergio. I feel so evil I start laying into Dad.

"Okay then, how much should we charge so you can spend quality time with your fantastic son? Fifty euros an hour? You have plenty of money, don't you? What do you need it for? Are you going to take it to the grave? Do you need a nice inlay on your coffin?"

I'm using a heavy stone to squash some drink caps. Dad comes over beaming, and says he wants to take a photo of me, but I feel such a mess inside and out. I'm finding it hard to breathe through my nose. It's hard to keep my mouth closed when I chew. Generally not feeling well. Grandma says to cheer up, it's a party after all. "Never look a gift horse, eh?"

"I don't really think of Dad as a gift horse. He has never brought any joy to me."

"Heena, come on, maybe your future bright, eh? I read your fortune in tea leaves. You make us all a cup. Brighten up everything, eh?"

Better to escape to the kitchen, for five minutes of peace.

"Heena, the leaves tell me the future seem decided,

but you can still change your mind. Is the sort of decision easily made, yet easy to undo if you've made mistake. Yet every leaf bleeding from the tiny holes enclosing them is saying, 'You'll pay.'"

"And that's meant to cheer me up?"

Dad brushes back spit-black hair and states, "Note that, Heena. Lift art above your head, and train your inner brat."

He's trying to be clever. Grandma seems to be really enjoying playing the hostess. Dad's determined to get a photo of us all, and tries to get everyone together. It's difficult to get everyone settled, and then, just when we are, Grandma disappears upstairs to change out of her white outfit into black. We're trying to call her back because she looks great, but she carries on up the stairs. Dad says he really wants me in the photo because he doesn't have one of me.

"Like you care about that, Dad."

Grandma says "You have a handsome and understanding father. You have no reason to hate him."

Dad's wild and unpredictable. He makes sporadic attempts to be a responsible father, and for weeks at a time can seem happy to raise two children, but soon realises it's a trap of his own devising. Well, I no longer feel I have to be in the trap with him, my cage door is open. I see it and I can walk out, though no one thinks I can.

I decide to leave this party right now, no one can make me stay. I see Grandma sorting everyone out with a plate of bread, cheese and cherry tomatoes. The ground is wet so she puts down rubber car mats, then drags out a table and chairs for everyone. People are talking at the top of their voices, and Grandma's happy because she has created a sort of habitable place from the scrubby old garden.

I'm not proud to feel my feelings, and can't express them out loud without causing war amongst family and friends. No one would be on my side. I'm the ugly gnome in the middle of the lawn, viciously staring into big open space. That's how mean I feel. As I leave to catch the bus, I watch how the rain bounces off Grandma's arms, which are still filled with tat as she hurries everyone inside. I'm so relieved when the bus arrives.

I dream I'm choosing, and persuading someone to fit orgasm seats. I want mine fitted immediately. They're held with expanding bolts, have a round seat, and are amazing! There are also clothes and tons of shoes being brought out for sale. I design huge easels, made from massive cranes. Someone comes up and hacks into my hair for the camera. Other people have fancy stuff, but we're sharing a toothbrush. Someone has really upset Mum and I'm comforting her. I pee into this huge empty suitcase, and someone walks in.

I wake up at 8.40 am, overwhelmingly sad after a dream about my mum. She's going somewhere and the pretext is to take my ouija board. It's going to be for a few days with a tea tray and knitting and it just seems so sad and hopeless.

I've been thinking about what makes people hurt others the way they do. My mother and father have never even considered what I might want or need, they just get on with their selfish lives regardless.

Truthfully, I prefer to be around animals, Sabe and Kipper with their furry little, burr-filled bodies, Siam's snaggleteeth, Nonny and his fandango, Guacamole and his lizard discretion and discrimination, poking out of his hide when he hears the rustle of a locust. I watch my fish calmly swim through his dinosaur skull, until I approach with food and he whips back and forth in a frenzy. I imagine examining a cranium in the way my fish does, swimming through the eyes and open jaws, through the ear canal, and nesting in the cave of an absent tongue. Entering the nasal cavity, leaving through a hole in the top of the cranium.

Aaron

A party invitation arrives with a badge included, which says, 'Jerk off at Number 10', and it's from Ashish. So, here I am, holding court in the hallway chair, slopping more wine on my underwear even as my clothes are tumbling in the dryer. Although he invited me to the party, when I arrive Ashish is chatting up some man. I'm surprised to see the guy isn't attractive he's squat and dumpy. Ashish takes the glass from my hand and passes it to the guy, who takes a swig and then puts it down somewhere just as the fire alarm goes off, and we all trail outside. It's obvious some idiot has set it off, and there's no fire, but the man won't go back and get my drink. I start really laying into him, being abusive, and he's laughing about it.

* * *

I realise everyone's having a meat feast. They're passing round chops and salami, *et cetera*, and eating nothing else. There's a big keg of lager on the table. Jill is there, and she tries to get me to sit down. She starts talking about her two children, both gay. We're on a sofa, with a heater on one side and I help myself to lager. Jill says, "I'll have some too," but her glass is black, filthy because cigarette butts have been put out in it, and it looks so vile I can't imagine getting it clean enough to drink out of.

She seems very sad, and I wonder why. I become upset, and start crying, so she puts her arm around me. I'm afraid she's psychic and knows something has happened to my mum. She starts stroking my hair, and doesn't seem put off by how filthy it is.

I'm going to nip out to buy a pack of ten cigarettes so I can roll a joint, but remember I have a pack I found at the bus stop, laying around somewhere in my bag. I am distracted by Jill's attention, and her arm around me, and accidentally set fire to the corner of the match box instead of lighting the joint.

Jill says "Aaron, my son always does that."

I say "I wonder if it's a symptom of being gay?" because I'm starting to feel a bit out of it.

* * *

I start talking to two women sat behind me, and someone starts handing out food on little bits of toast. I speak to them in Spanish and explain it is all 'carne' and I can't eat meat. Another guy offers me something from another tray and I explain again that it is meat, but he's insistent, and then he says, "No one's eating enough, sadly."

I go to the front to take my turn at the microphone, but some guy, a dwarf, is playing a loud instrument in the room. I try talking over him at first, and everyone's smiling. Then I go up to him and start doing a crazy dance in time to the music, and he starts dancing too.

Ashish brings me wine in an amazing glass and I'm so anxious the stem snaps in my hand. I read my poem:

Thirteen Ways of Looking at Beetles

Beetles know a huge percentage of erections aren't caused by desire, so standing on top of a skyscraper is to be astride a city built from fear.

Six beetles watching two women fight are reluctant to pull them apart, because this is what the movies tell them they've been waiting for all their lives.

A beetle realises the danger of releasing himself onto an abject world where people tightly cork their pleasures in bottles in case they ever need to get them off the shelf.

A beetle likes the cold and empty solitude of vodka. The woman prefers the warmth of frothy beer. His afternoon face is scratching her, his tongue, all muscle, is a dead weight. A lump of meat which he moves slowly.

A beetle measures time seeing soap shrink in the dish, and already wants to dress her in yum-yum yellow, before lowering her into shark-infested waters.

In Italy, a beetle shoots at a woman for taking a bunch of grapes from his vineyard, Then, laughing, opens his truck door to her and drives all night to Poggi Bonsi, where beetles follow her in packs when she ventures out alone.

A beetle realises he's growing old when, amongst the collection of guns and knives stored under his sofa, he finds one he used to use to cut the telephone cords in women's flats.

A beetle gets a pram for his 21ˢᵗ birthday and does two clumsy things for his son: he knits a cardigan with two too-long sleeves, and carves a wooden horse.

A beetle stands in his Formica kitchen, the pinnacle of his achievement, plastic wood pushed into all the scars and scuffs of his embedded temper.

A beetle leaves a woman instructions for her working day: Dear Slave, spoke-shave the wagon wheel, strip the chairs, stain the grain on John Cleese's table, Love Master.

A beetle's neckerchief gets caught in the belt-sander, and he escapes strangling only because it's made of silk.

Without balls, the beetle wears the tightest briefs, though he still jiggles the change in his jeans pocket as a substitute. He's not sorry to lose that cock which can no longer smirk at Him.

A beetle is unsure of how to deal with her 'fuck me' heels. He fantasises her marching amongst an army of long, slender legs, some of them grazed from kneeling down in front of him. But he doesn't know if he wants her to press the heel into his chest, or fall over herself getting away from him.

* * *

I walk into the bathroom, where various people are blasting out music. I decide to have a bath, though I'm a bit worried Ashish won't know where I am and might think I've disappeared. He follows me in, rubs cocaine into my gums, and then climbs into the bath. When we leave, someone comments on how loud we were, and offers a smoky kiss, which I refuse because it would take away the taste of Ashish. Sex has been my usual route to feeling anything, and I'm sorry it often doesn't matter who it is. It's a way to make contact with myself, or to lose myself some place. I never want to stay around the person who has taken me on that journey, whose body I've used. Except this time. I think I've found someone I can also stand to be around.

When everyone finally starts leaving, I can't see Ashish or Jill, and I call out to ask if anyone's going for the bus; "Please, I don't know where it leaves from."

A very sexy woman, who I recognise as one of the artists from *Fallout* comes up to me. She has one eye made up heavily, and bright red lips. She takes my hand and leads me to the door. As we leave, I hand my gum to some guy, as I walk past him and he looks surprised, and I say, "Oh sorry, that should've been for your Dad." He stands there, holding the sticky gum between his fingers, and I think, *Oh God, I'm taking revenge for some guy sticking gum in my hand months ago. How much have I drunk, and what's going to happen now?*

I forgot my bag, but don't want to go back into the party because it would be embarrassing. I decide I won't need it tonight – my keys are in my jacket pocket. Someone follows us out and asks where I live, and it feels threatening. My shoes feel like loose rags around my feet, and I can hardly walk. I think about finding a phone box and ringing someone to pick me up.

I feel lost, at a dead end.

I walk along with the sexy artist, who sees two women she says are after her. We hide in a garbage dumpster. I realise I'm a natural coward and feel thoroughly ashamed. Maybe I just need life to throw the opportunity to be brave at me.

PART THREE

You can hallucinate tiny rocks into a lunar landscape, the sun is that fierce, shadows that intense and three-dimensional. Umbrellas are for shade, dogs for guarding, and cats for target practice. On the crescent curve, the mysteries of lizard, snake, tarantula, and praying mantis are trodden underfoot, as women lug home potatoes and onions to make tortilla.

Diana

Catalina's dead.

She was visiting her parents on their island when she got knocked down with no witnesses to the hit and run. Heena and Sergio will go to live at Pilar's for now, while Miguel remains at the villa. We've decided the children shouldn't attend the funeral. I'm the only one travelling by plane, because Miguel doesn't trust the tiny eight-seater connecting the mainland to the islands, and so he travels by boat.

If Pilar had been welcome at the funeral I'm sure she would've said, "That plane's like travel on hairdryer."

Before take-off I see the pilot stumble over the hill, and we climb on board via a shaky rope platform, which is raised to the height of the doorway. Quite a primitive method.

I can never decide if I love or hate the speed of being a plane passenger. It makes me philosophical, realising ultimately that life's out of my hands, even though I take the controls sometimes. An invisible pilot makes the major moves. As Miguel once put it, "Life's like putting your bollocks inside the jaws of a crocodile but getting killed by a bee sting."

I feel like a pinhole camera, with everything turned upside down inside me. Or shaken, like my favourite cocktail, to settle in green and blue stripes. Clouds are sticky wet, and I know the plane can hover just as safely below them as above, but it doesn't feel that way.

After the rush of Granada city, it's a shock to encounter the lull of the island and its three uninhabitable humps. The ancient ruins are hidden until you get up close. As your feet take you over the hill top, you see rising before you, a hidden sandstone circle. Imagine the slaves piling up the sandstones, a heap of misery, with sweat and blood mixed in.

I know I'm taking a risk meeting Miguel on this island, with the ghost of my rival everywhere. The ocean seems to bob with the tide of Catalina, and when it turns I feel she's getting up to leave because I've arrived. There are things I should talk to Miguel about, but if he thinks not, then I'll take the easy route, and won't contradict him.

There's a gap within the clouds as they roll over the thinnest moment of sea meets air; it's like a coma, suspended and ready to re-animate with the right conditions at exactly the right time. I remember dragging Catalina through these fields, which hold their bobble heads high, trembling lightly on a breeze, stepping into a bog which only our feet knew about. Right now I want to be at Pilar's house, lively with Heena and Sergio.

I walk to the villa, to give myself time to acclimatise. Crunching over loose chippings, I walk for an hour, eyes alert, jumping into the hedges filled with life, to avoid traffic that doesn't expect someone to walk beside the narrow tarmac strip. My artist's eyes look inward, the soles of my feet remembering.

Waves roll in from the island – violent and urgent waves which rock a gentle boat, straining at the rope tying it to the buoy. The fast channel appears, fast track for shells and debris. Miguel tells me that on the morning of his wedding, he took a swim, and the sea froze his bladder so much he couldn't pee all day. Do testicles really jump back inside, frightened by the cold?

Children are collecting sea creatures in buckets. I wonder at the future of a planet in hands so careless - they wrench limpets from their safe place and leave them to dry out, saying, "It's all right, there are millions of them." Do I even believe in time as linear?

Miguel says "There's no separate past, present, and future. Creature Earth has baby legs at the front and its old person legs at the back, and is happy to chase its tail in circles."

Thoughts around Catalina's accident are tumbling around in my mind. Such a beautiful place to find yourself dying, but inconvenient for everyone having to fly out here. She would've hated that. Catalina loved being a mother, and deserved it more than many who throw away the chance of spending proper time with their child.

I remember the last time I was here with Catalina, only weeks before I found out she was fucking Miguel. We decided to hitch-hike the length of the island, and quickly realised there's an etiquette in hitch-hiking, like at a taxi rank, where the car pulls up at the front of the queue and takes the first hitcher, rather than being selective.

It can be a long wait. Catalina and I decided to speed up our journey, so we took turns hiding behind the bushes, while the other stood a little removed from the crowd, in hot pants and vest. Before long a guy ignored the line of hitchers and opened the door of his low slung sports car for me.

We both felt so alive, and so close that day. We were so close that when Miguel told me he had got Catalina pregnant, I felt the loss of her friendship more than the loss of my trust in Miguel. More betrayed by her than by him, because I've always known Miguel's weakness and depravity. His lack of conscience was no surprise. For a while I even imagined I might be able to stay friends with Catalina, help her raise the child. But I realised I'm not able to divide myself in the way Miguel and Catalina apparently can.

* * *

Today is solemn.

On reaching the villa, I watch the window arches replay their rosy hue over and over again. Catalina replaced the lemon clouds of stained glass glorification with panes of clear glass, so a full, clear light shines over the hidden mystery of the roses outside and, further away, the sea. Writ large is a subtext of angels sleeping.

The roses Catalina brought indoors are still leaking onto the table from the cracked earthenware vase she arranged them in. The fissure is invisible but it must be there because a streak of cold perspiration slowly descends into a pool. I can feel my insect bites, with the raised skin itching, and I apply some of the cool water to my neck and forehead.

Miguel is intent on persuading me to go back to live at the villa with him. He says there's a building I could convert into an art studio on the grounds. I've always dreamt of having my own studio, being able to work in solitude, making work in every kind of material, and having my quiet thoughts play alongside my ideas.

I've enjoyed my art space at *Fallout*, but I'm always being dragged into tedious dramas with everyone from the *Fallout* company. Not only that, everyone constantly finds an excuse to hang around chatting when I have an idea for a piece, and I'm aware of an imminent deadline.

More annoyingly, even though they have a designer in place, they frequently ask me for help with the set building. I have a device, which drops paint from above, like a rectangular shower. One of the company will come over, and ask, "Could you just paint this?" The object might be the size of a bed stood on its end, and I have to mix paint and fill the shower, then move the object into the right place, wasting time I don't have.

"Diana, it's so satisfying watching the mixing, like a magic trick as the white powder turns to black liquid."

So Miguel's offer is very tempting and, naturally,

being a magician, he has more tricks up his sleeve.

"Dee, the villa's only a few miles from the foundry. We can buy a van to take your work for casting. It's what you always wanted. We can afford it now."

I imagine all the worlds that would open up for me. I could carve sculptures in wax and polystyrene, cast them into brass, bronze, and aluminium. Drag the metal pieces up from the depths of the huge sand pit, like visions from hell – red, hot and twisted. I could hang them on butcher's hooks to cool in eerie tableau and push through them like curtains of meat. Imagine the scale and the permanence, instead of the fragile and ephemeral pieces I've made to date. They wouldn't even scratch at the surface of art history.

* * *

When I came to the island, I didn't expect to find Miguel trapped on a slope while pain rolls over and over him. He asked me to marry him, a practical step. So I'll never have to provide evidence in court against him. I wouldn't have to stand in a witness box and say: "I saw Miguel take pleasure in murdering two innocent people, and then I helped him hide the evidence."

He deludes himself that what he did was for the good of society, but isn't stupid enough to think a judge would see it that way. Going back to Miguel would be a step towards pretending it never happened, but I'll never marry Miguel, even if I would be safer by doing so.

The other question I can't shut down in my mind: do I think Miguel killed Catalina? His coke-fuelled killing of a gay couple, his hatred of homosexuals, his high states, and his stupid responses when high, doesn't mean he's capable of coldly calculating the death of someone he loved, and who had his child. He has threatened that if I don't let him back into my life he'll kill me, but a threat thrown out in desperation to swing someone's judgement is very far from carrying out the threat. Isn't it?

Miguel felt Catalina didn't respect him, but I'm sure their relationship was kept alive by the friction between them, as was ours. On the other hand, there's the possibility she had found someone else and really was intent on leaving him. That she had woken up one day and was no longer prepared to wait around for him to honour her with a little of his time. It's hard not to feel resentful of being at his beck and call when he doesn't even care enough to call and say if he'll be home.

If she left him he would've lost out on her villa and money. It's probably her wealth was all he wanted from her; that, and Sergio. Miguel says she deserved what she got. I can't believe she would leave without taking Sergio, but I also believe Miguel would've done anything to stop her leaving with him.

Of course, Catalina didn't deserve to die but she is living on by Miguel constantly talking about her, even if it is mostly in bitter rants. She had the power to hurt him, I can see that, but unless Miguel drops this mass of destructive hate, he's keeping alive the worst of her. He's angry because he doesn't know who held her most, who she really cared for. He says she didn't deserve his love, or Sergio's, but he's competing for an affection, which can no longer be had or proved.

* * *

The decision has been made.

The opportunity for my own studio won. I arrange to talk to Tila before the others about my plan to leave *Fallout*, because I'm aware of how insecure she feels whenever there are any changes around her, especially anyone leaving.

When I meet up with her in our favourite restaurant, without the interference of anyone else's presence, it's as though all the dramas of the last months have never happened, and Tila's so happy it's hard telling her my plans. I open my wallet to pay for our first drink, and see the photo of Heena held against my thighs, at a party. I also have a bunch of dried herbs, very recently sent to me, to remind me that the same hands which held Heena took the wheel of a red *Volkswagen Beetle* while its previous occupants were treated like the remains of a picnic, left for the wolves.

Outside the restaurant, an area of scrubby grass car park is sticky with red and smashed glass. Someone complains about ruining their canvas shoes on the broken jars of pasta sauce. I grow cold to the depth of my bones and I hear my stupid voice say, "We have to clear it up." The wine bottle smashing on the rock was the only violent part; the knife slipped in so easily it was a silent and, apparently, natural act. No one murmured. The boy watching the dying man, transfixed as the knife was quietly turned on him. The seep of blood and wine is what I remember most.

* * *

Heena being back at Pilar's doesn't prevent Miguel getting her to perform as a magician in order to sell his snake oil. It's one thing Miguel wasting his life as a snake oil merchant, but I know Heena deserves better. I've been on the wrong side of Heena ever since I moved into my studio at the villa. She's by no means easy, but I want her to believe it's not all my fault. I didn't want her to go to live with Catalina and Miguel. I know how hard she finds it to be moved back and forth.

"Heena, it's easier to shout and be angry at my solid flesh than at the unfairness which slaps us all down."

"Let me guess, Mum, you call it fate."

"Well whatever it's called, something seems to hand out the most unlikely pain to one person, and give a much happier combination for another."

"Mum, you blame everyone and everything but yourself. If you wanted me, Dad would've had to put up with it. Since when do you do what he orders you to do?"

I know Heena's hurting when all she seems to want to do is put me down. She wants to be loved at her worst and constantly tests me, angry even when I prove I can. She uses her tiny knuckle of power against me, small rabbit punches. She knows how to hurt me with a small jab, withdraw, small jab, withdraw, at just the right time so it does its job.

* * *

This is what I dream last night and I wonder how to interpret it:

I roll under the wheels of an oil tanker and snake my body as it's swept into the air. Then I grab hold of a handle, which mysteriously appears on the smooth tank and try to time it exactly so I'm not crushed underneath.

* * *

I squeeze out my colours and stack my greasy crayons. The oil fumes are baked and trapped by the blistered door, adding a special kind of seeing to my sweeping arm strokes. Today's all about red. In England they call it brick red, here we call it English red, and the chimneys and walls tell the story of heat.

I'm choosing sculptures and paintings with Jan for my exhibition, some still in progress. She's most interested in the tiny figurative paintings and doesn't want to put in the larger ones which make it expensive to 'maintain'. We choose a number of the smaller, squarer paintings, and sculptures.

"Diana, my favourite series are these scary manipulative children. I also love these with the girl half-falling through the floor in all these different buildings. Your work has become very dark recently."

"Well you know I sold my soul for a bit of canvas, wood, and nails long ago."

"You need to get those sculptures back from *Fallout*

Studios, the exhibition ended months ago, and it would be good to show them alongside the paintings."

"I've tried. I'm expecting a total confrontation with Jill at some point, as she has been ignoring my phone calls and letters. I've been thinking about breaking in and taking them, but maybe I'll finally have to just go see her in person. She's still angry about me not giving notice when I stopped renting a space at *Fallout*. She turned against me and gave up on me when I stopped exhibiting there."

Tila turns up at my studio, practically tearing her hair out because she has been doing everything she can to make Jill fall in love with her, but Jill's being cold towards her, and seems to have totally broken off the friendship.

"Diana, everyone at Fallout's against me."

"Jill's so devoted to her work, the company."

Worryingly, it's apparent Tila's delusions are getting out of hand; in fact she seems to have lost her handle on reality. She has come off her medication again, either because it makes her feel dull, or she just forgot to pick it up. I want to help her, but at the same time I'm dealing with so much chaos, including pressure from Miguel.

"Tila, I don't have room for you to stay with me. There's hardly room for me to live as well as work here."

I walk her to the local bar and, as luck would have it, bump into Miguel. He's probably too drunk to travel far afield, and has made Heena set up to sell outside the village bar. She stands at the cloth-covered table, behind an open suitcase and, as we approach the bar, begins holding up small bottles and calling out, "Bring back love! Get rid of your rivals! Cure your pain!"

Heena immediately seats Tila and takes a bottle from the case. She rubs the oil into her hands and neck, places her hands on Tila's head and closes her eyes.

"Now your pains are gone! The cure lives in the bottle!"

She holds it in the air.

"Five Euros. Rub the medicine into your hands and neck twice a day."

"She cured me!" Tila says.

"Money will return to you a hundred fold! Change your luck! A loved one will return to you. Let my magic bring them back!"

"Diana, she'll bring my good luck back."

"You know Heena isn't a magician. She's being exploited by her drunk of a father. Miguel's nothing more than a snake oil merchant, preying on superstitious and lonely people."

"She's a spiritual healer."

"Tila. It's an act."

"She healed me."

"I'm getting us drinks."

As I go up to the bar, Tila's still insisting, "She might help."

Suddenly, she believes Heena to be the guru she's been looking for all her life. She's tired of being told she's unwell every time she has mystical experiences. She imagines she's found someone who can validate them.

Miguel holds out his hand to Heena for some Euros and comes up to the bar. Tila leans towards Miguel and confides, "In my own small way I'm a healer, too. For snakes, lizards, all the lives trodden underfoot. Everything deserves respect."

I nudge Tila away.

"Let's find somewhere more amenable."

She's on a roll now. "Strewn like rubbish. A rabbit nailed to a tree. A cat used for target practice."

"Heena, please can you take Tila back to your grandma's with you. She'll look after her. Miguel, Heena has to go now, so why don't you pack up? Go home and sleep it off."

Miguel

The only way to get on and off the island by foot is via a bridge. It's unmaintained, and falling apart. I watch a girl risk walking along the bridge, but she says, "It's becoming impossible to use, no longer even half planked. I stepped on a mess of plastic bottles and containers, which shifted and dropped down. If someone ever clears the rubbish from below there won't even be a bridge."

I say "Well if it's impossible, should we risk it and die?"

She says "We won't die. We aren't good enough people to die young."

"I'm not good, but it's impossible for you to know that."

"Miguel, I know all about you. Most of it is bad."

She grins and walks past me. I'm certain I've never seen her before in my life, and I wonder who has been talking, and what they said. Dee has an opinion about everything and would argue a point if she felt strongly about it. She's so clever. Catalina's different, not so smart but more persistent, more likely to gossip. Well, it seems I always bring out the harridan, the scold, in the women I love. Without meaning to, I inspire members of the female race to gallop forward with their wooden spoon raised to hurl peas at pain, and when I try to stop them, they want to cut steaks out of my eyes.

Catalina was never afraid of blood, not squeamish; when I talked about stepping off the boat and finding ourselves in a shark's stomach, she smiled.

"What sweet suicide, what a journey, to feel yourself as muscled as a tongue, as invincible as a second row of teeth."

In the restaurant I saw fish outgrowing the tank. Looking down at my hands, I noticed moss growing.

"Miguel, will we be safer when our flesh loses its firmness, and finally falls off the bones? Will we find another body, or will the spirit prove to be mind and assert itself in the process? Demand a less complicated set of feelings, and feel sure of at least one thing?"

I hope one day I might find my way into a fish, learn everything there is to know about water, the shoal, how it operates, how it feels to be separated from the surging waves, to find yourself in the still waters of a fish tank. Would I still feel the tug of the shoal? I often sit in front of a fish tank, stare at silvery scales, observing fish-writings, fish-thoughts.

When the restaurant tank cracked, a dozen fish tumbled onto the table, huge and thrashing. All their previous lives poked out of their jaws and gills. A tumbler floated on the surface of the water, another sank, and the tablecloth became a sail, spoons were oars, chopsticks masts. I felt I had been here before.

Sluice gates opened and we were swept down flooded streets, dolphins raised their glasses and passed a peace pipe. Clouds with feet sticking out, were black booted, an army, above a sea of frothy red, cheeky *Vimto*.

Catalina saw me open my breast as sanctuary for sinners, saw them beating on the door for cures, in exchange for payment. She had money enough for both of us, but what man would let a woman pay for him? A man needs independence, and Catalina would never give me sufficient money for drugs and beer. She provoked me into throwing a fish-spatula at her.

"Miguel, you've ruined everything with your violence. You cut my face and won't even apologise. You have to leave."

"Why should I leave? I did nothing wrong. What will you gain if you cast me out? If you leave, I'll hunt you down and destroy you. Catalina, you think you're so strong, fighting me in every way, but I'll kill you. Now are you afraid?"

Pilar

I so sorry for Sergio that his mum dead, but he far from being alone. Heena make him see-saw, smooth green plank see-saw that go so high, he can see whole world from up there. I give him all my attention.

Is winter and we get cold from being out on the see-saw, so when we get home, I light a fire under the kitchen table. We pull blanket over our knees and is hot and cosy under. When it get dark, buffet become Sergio's taxi, and he park it under the table and play with bag of marbles, which he say are family of fish.

When it bed time, I throw him over my shoulder, because I coal man, and he sack of coal. I tip him onto bed, switch on lamp, make shadows and tell stories.

Is same care I give Heena when she small. School terrible for her, because Señora Rodriguez old and mean, and keep red and yellow plastic bats for punishment. She make kids choose which bat they whacked with, but if they choose yellow she use red. So I let Heena skip school. She much happier being with me and helping mix medicines for Miguel to sell.

Sergio decide box room where he sleep is haunted. He terrify himself by going into room, which he say full of rustling and moaning sounds. Then he pretend to have ear ache, so he cuddle up with me on bed settee and watch musical shows.

Heena bring warm flannel to me so I wash my hands and face before cup of tea. I keep soda under my bed, and is my secret, but if Sergio feel brave he steal a swig or two.

Whenever I produce pack of playing cards, Heena's

happy, because this is passion we share. I read cards and will tell anyone their fortune for a little money. I teach my children and grandchildren card game and tricks when they're big enough. Sometimes use match sticks to bet, but money whenever someone give me chance.

* * *

Is Sergio's birthday, and Heena scowling because of course she too old for party games young ones enjoy, and she have to help with children. Children build creatures out of food, I put on music, and we make fiesta, rush out onto the streets.

Food creature is game I try many times before, and find so difficult. I have pile of eggs, soft-boiled, almost bursting. I trying bear-creature but remember amazing lizard Heena capture and put in a bucket. She say it feel cruel, but was injured and show us wide cut, horizontal on upper biceps.

Heena say "Is asking be set free."

It clinging to toy like raft.

* * *

Today we bandy words and I say Dee a useless mother, and I know I hurt Heena. Dee send Sergio a duvet with horns and clothes hangers which are two-headed monsters.

My older son, Juan, come over from Madrid and take me and Sergio to market. Sergio pick up weird wooden head on a snake's body which undulate, and show it to Juan, and he buy it for Sergio. Is thirty euro.

Then a second thing Sergio pick up and Juan buy for him, another thirty euro. When he does it with third thing I'm furious.

I say "Juan, you can't keep buy everything rubbish. We need buy proper thing like bread."

I ask him for twenty-five euros for help with party, and he say, "Again! You look thin, lose lot of weight."

I say "I not dieting."

He say "You drinking."

I say what a hypocrite he his, with his politic about poor people, when he care nothing about me. I stay away from people mean and judgemental, stick to people like me, not much money.

Tila

I dream I'm showing off for Diana, feeding my addiction for apples, which I eat throughout. I steal some when we aren't served for ages. I'm behind her and touching her until we start snogging. I realise her gums are disintegrating, with pieces of flesh, gums, and tooth remaining in my mouth. She says she wants to stop because she's panicking about losing a tooth, but she has lost all of them and I give her a handful back. I'm spitting out bits of flesh and blood as I go along. I smash a big mirror. It's the third time I have smashed one. I eat a big oaty biscuit, which tastes like life.

* * *

I've always felt good in this shirt, worn with tight *Levis*, a silver belt, and a waistcoat. There's a kind of sanctuary for me in the punk stripe of this waistcoat. I'm wearing it with a black tail-coat, when I finally hook Jill. Her wedding invitation, sealed in its manila envelope, was the Queen of Spades card.

I have a blast watching Ashish marry Aaron. They leave the wedding party early and, as the sky turns dark with night striding in, I fall drunkenly out of a tree and crack a rib laughing at Jill chatting up a boy she already knows what it would be like to fuck.

When she finally collects her riding boots to leave, I go over to hug her and an electric bolt jolts me. I'm certain there's a message contained within thigh meets thigh, and I feel a new crackle in my step. I'm a moth, heading for the moon, when suddenly someone shines a torch, and I'm dragged right off course, even if that light wasn't intended for me.

I follow Jill out of the park, and suddenly we're kissing outside the fruit shop, and she tells the staring giggling girls, "It's okay, we're sisters."

Helpful.

It's very sexy being desired by Jill; I'm so attracted to her. We race back to mine, with her stealing chocolates and cheese for us to have for dinner. She puts them in my pockets. She feeds me avocados, to calm me, and strokes a playing card she thinks looks like me.

In the early hours, she starts to remove my clothes.

I've often watched Ashish and Aaron doing their same show-off dance moves, looking exactly alike, Ashish flirting with Aaron, so happy and extroverted. But now I have Jill, I'm no longer jealous.

* * *

Jill paints my kitchen yellow, and it's strange, because it had never occurred to me to do up the place. It's a revelation. The only things I've seen in Jill's fridge are vodka, grapefruit, and pudding. Occasionally Jamaican raisin bread and processed cheese, prepared on a bread board which serves as a plate, brushed clean afterwards.

I introduce cooking into her life. She cracks open my gas meter with bolt cutters, so we can use the same coin over and over again. Today, making dinner, I break the remaining egg into her soup and stir it in, stabbing it quite viciously with a knife. I wish I'd made it for myself, as it's suddenly just what I fancy eating.

"Jill, what's the longest you've been with a partner, because all the women I meet seem to have gone out with their partner for years?"

"I was with my children's father for four years, but that was many years ago. I cannot imagine repeating the experience."

I'm sure I can change her mind.

* * *

Being with her makes me feel alive, confident, after weeks of depression. I can imagine dancing on stage again, wearing a mile-high dress. I would make it myself out of folded and cut paper.

I long to make my presence known again, so I go back to *Fallout* and join in the contemporary dance class. I find my body is fit and supple, which I hadn't expected it to be. I start doing an acrobatic twisting and taking off, twisting parallel to the ground, in mid-air, and it feels amazing and familiar.

* * *

I'm covered in red shoe dye from a bottle of liquid I picked up in someone's art space. It's staining my fingers. I feel a bit in the way. Jill and Ashish are here but I've positioned myself so they can't see me. Still, I can hear their conversation. Ashish says he was with Maria and she sneaked something from someone's bin.

Some old woman came out to criticise them for the way they were behaving, hanging outside laughing and talking. Maria yelled at her, "It's none of your fucking business."

* * *

So, things haven't changed much during my absence. Well, some things have. I feel invisible. Jill's giving out whatever equipment everyone needs, but I'm saying, "Can't you see me?"

My desk is now covered with all kinds of junk and impossible to get to. Jill has invited Perry to join the group and says there's room for another desk for him.

She's talking to someone, vaguely and unenthusiastically raising a hand when she sees me. When she goes out she complains about me to the others, and I confront her when she comes back in. She's on the phone, clutching a see-through bag stuffed with coins. She says everyone's helping with something: the pile of washing up is done, glasses clean, a couple drinking a last bottle of wine are tidying everything.

"You should be helping clear up, Tila. Help move some furniture."

"I can't help, Jill, I have plans. You can see my injury."

"I can't."

She's wearing trousers the same colour as her CPPP jacket and when I choose to say I hate the colour of them, all hell breaks loose. I become shrewish, screaming at her.

She calls "Tila."

I say "Bitch," and walk off.

She comes after me, going on about a funeral, and then she's once again threatening to clear out of the studios and leave us all to it.

No one is on my side. There's no one I can trust, and I have no idea what I did wrong.

* * *

We're sharing the lighting designer with one of the other companies, there's very little time for plotting, and we're expecting a great audience, interesting people, for this last night. Somehow the props we use for the opening segment have disappeared. The matinee audience are coming in, and we don't know how to start it. I can usually improvise, but today I feel defeated, and wonder who sabotaged everything.

When I open the big gate, the other performers think I'm opening the door to start the show. Someone says 'Thank you,' and they all begin to troop out.

The door's still half-closed, but there's no stopping them now, so I have to fully open it and let them go. It's a huge arena and I see the vast crowd of people watching. I race after the others, but they're pulling ahead and I feel like I'm running cross-legged. Two of us are far behind and take a short-cut, and I see a rhinoceros enter between two walls.

* * *

Outside, I notice two strange aircraft, huge and remote-controlled. Sometimes one seems much bigger than the other, which confuses me. Some guys are playing a game of rugby in the main road. I have an ironing board, because we're on the endless parade of preparation for the next show. I start pumping up a balloon and when it bursts there isn't time to have another go, but I want to take one with me. When I've done everything I turn out the light, and see a small snake opening its mouth wide. I feel life could spiral downhill, I feel the presence of pressures in my life, which could become unbearable. I need clarity of mind and insight. A red planet lands on a covered bit of garden, only just missing me. I remember on an earlier occasion a grey meteor has landed just there. I use an extending ladder to climb up and look. There's already a big step-ladder being used and someone moves it out of my way so I can get through. Things are being dropped from the sky for us, like supplies. We're batting at wasps or bees, which are attacking us, and I start freaking out when they turn into a huge tiger. When I tell Jill she won't believe me.

"Jill, just because nothing amazing happens in your life, you won't believe when it happens in mine."

A man's body has turned into a big melted pool. His head's on top of the heap. His wife's complaining he has lost his appetite. He might be an MP. I start going through boxes of books to check for bombs.

* * *

I'm in a place where two armies train, and only a painted line divides the two training grounds. A cat walks out unscathed. I look in the mirror and I have no pubic hair. I look again, and still have none. Different kinds of seeds are used to represent words. They have to grow and can be sprouted first to help this process. Four of us have been told to sell fruit in cups. I ladle mine into about four cups from the bowl and lay them out to sell and drink the delicious cold juice. The others come back and have deliberately broken their cups in various ways. We're laughing over the reasons and ways they did it, especially one guy who has reluctantly destroyed a precious cup. We're laughing, saying it was Jesus' own cup.

Someone asks if I'm sleeping. We had been letting geese go right near the road, and they were following after us, and almost getting run over. I thought one of them was squashed in the road when I saw the ghost girl, still rolling into and out of her body.

* * *

I have to hide a piece of evidence about my person, and somehow get away from where the crime happened. I've killed someone and this item proves it. I have to find a better place, but I've lost my glasses somewhere, so I'm half-blind. There are queues of people leaving. Someone asks if I've seen Diana and I say no, though I'm not sure if it's her I've killed. I hope it isn't, but how can I be certain?

I sense anger towards me because the process I advised, using oiled charcoal, ruined her work. It ran amok and filled in the areas where she had done her careful pencil lines. To tell the truth, I think it looks amazing. Really, I do.

* * *

The whole of the basement is filled with clear water. I realise if the water enters more than it leaves, the water will rise up into the flat. I can't get hold of Diana on the phone, but when I get into the pool someone else is waiting for me.

The house is completely red inside, and sandstone textured. I walk through the rooms, some with small square rooms high up in them, then find I can't push the door open to get out because it's practically a whole wall.

Filled With Ghosts

I go back the way I came.

A small red killer, a lobster with teeth, escapes. Later, when I'm petting it in a box, it looks like another creature, a green lizard maybe. It escapes again, and people are still out to kill it.

* * *

We sleep on ground with deep chasms surrounding us, and the place I've chosen has water at head and foot. I think it's dangerous and want to extend the earth area. Someone offers some of theirs, but when I realise other people are sleeping on ground just as uneven and sometimes so small it only reaches their knees, I decide to be satisfied with what I have.

The creature ends up choked and squeezed to death. It's hard to kill. I can see various examples of transformation and metamorphosis and I know it is not good to kill the lizard, which is evoking creativity and primal instincts. It's like watching a film, and at a certain point the monster escapes and people are no longer passive. They might have doubts about killing it, but they're caught up in the idea of it.

* * *

I see a circle drawn on the ground with bombs going off all around it, dropped from above. Heena's in the circle, the bomb target, and when someone says we have to get her out of there, I roll her out and keep rolling. We become separated and I wonder how I can find her because I'm on a thin stretch of bridge, which was once the city. More bombs are dropped from the sky, then stick out of the ground. I try to defuse a big one, before I'm whisked away in a vehicle at the last second.

* * *

I hold a tiny bird, I hold it with its head peeping out and I'm going, "I've got a bird, I've got a bird," to Diana. It suddenly really grips my finger and it hurts, so I let it go.

We're talking about sex and she says some weird thing about Jill.

I say "She's like a cow in the midden. I would rather knit for half an hour."

Diana sings "Jealous!"

* * *

Heena's lizard escapes out of a gap when she closes the sliding window and she asks me to help her catch it. She has a box of live locusts and tries to put one into the vivarium, and they escape everywhere. They're massive, dark. Hundreds of them are covering the doors and walls. Her dog and cat both start eating them, but within seconds the locusts have eaten into, and destroyed, everything. There's nibbled polystyrene everywhere. I spot the lizard and pick him up to put him back in the vivarium, and he's massive, crocodile sized but pink-bellied. I get him to hang over the edge of the vivarium, and he swings from his arm pits, so I heave him over the side, which is difficult because it's so high above me. I yell for Heena as I'm scooping up handfuls of locusts trying to get them in the tank.

"You have to come here and help me."

I can't imagine how I can ever get them back.

When I exclaim to Heena at how massive they are she says, "Do you think it's you who has shrunk?"

* * *

People are running in the street and shotguns leave a trail of smoke, which I think might be poisonous. Someone says "I hope they shoot that down before it gets too close," and I see a green army tank in the sky, almost directly overhead. When they shoot it, it slides over me. I'm not crushed, but trapped under a corner.

I think, *That's exactly what I dreamt, and it's actually happened.*

I'm lost in tents, taken by bears, and swallowed by

snakes. Rusty springs spill time, and safety jackets hang uselessly from hooks.

You aren't safe.

None of us are safe.

Amber flashes relentlessly, long muscles and wasted limbs coil and endlessly spool.

Heena

I'm outside the bar when Tila wanders in with her shirt tied from shoulder to waist like a papoose. She carries a plate with toast and a jar of jam, which she puts on the table next to her.

She spreads out playing cards and begins writing on them. She informs the papoose, "This is the beginning. Every card has a story to tell and a scattered pack means anything can happen."

She stares intently at the jam. "Yellow jam. Does it mean I'm a fascist... or are they telling me that they're fascists? They should make it clear."

She looks down at her clothes.

"This T-shirt's the problem." She pulls off her shirt and red T-shirt, and starts plucking at my clothes, shoving the papoose at me.

"I need your help."

She takes something out of her shirt, which turns out to be a dead kitten. I try to get her inside the bar, saying, "If you bring the kitten in we can give it milk."

She strokes the kitten, and says, "I won't let them harm you. Indoors everything's red hot. Electrified."

"Bring him in now, Tila."

She shouts "I can't!"

Dad wanders outside and says, "Hey, lady, do you need meat for your kitty to build up his strength? Would you like a nice bag of shot sparrow? I can shoot some for you. Bang! They will be dead!"

* * *

I've had enough of Tila, and however much Mum wants to shove her off on other people, Tila's supposed to be her friend.

I go over to the villa and bang on her studio door. "Hola, Heena! You got a day off? Is Daddy sleeping off his beer?" We sit down on a bench.

"We worked late last night bottling and labelling."

"Oh, I've had plenty of opportunities to see Miguel bottling. He empties more bottles down his neck than he fills. Did you get any chance to study this week?"

"Well, I read a book."

I hand her the battered paperback, *The Magus of Strovolos. The Extraordinary World of a Spiritual Healer.*

"It's Tila's. This book contains the crap she believes in, and Mum it's impossible to do anything with her around. She's constantly harassing me. You should talk to her. She thinks I'm some sort of guru, and that I can save her life."

"Well yes. She's petty unwell."

"She's imagining all kinds of things are going to happen to me. Thinks I'm in serious trouble, with a manhunt aiming to drag me off to be tortured somewhere."

"Christ. Christ. I'll go and see her."

"Talk to Dad too, he's driving me mad. Totally relies on me to do the selling."

"He can do his own selling. He used to when you were small. He takes advantage of you now you're older, that's all."

"He is drinking more now. Sometimes he can hardly stand. No one would buy a cure from him."

"He needs a cure, and you need to get out of his shadow. You're not responsible for him."

* * *

Dinner at Grandma's is invariably pea and potato soup –
bright green. Her house is a wreck, but has a cool garden
surrounding a big covered courtyard. She's fuming that
they sold the house next door, which stood empty for
years, because she fantasised about buying it one day,
joining it to hers, and creating a ghastly extended family
home. Grandma's house always seems to be in the
condition of being re-decorated, and the discomfort of
stepping over damp, shredded, white-wash, sweeping it
up, and slapping it back on, in an endless cycle. Every
room's tackled in sequence, and by the time the last strip
has been daubed, it's time to go back to the beginning
and start stripping again.

Grandma, half drunk, can often be found hanging
over the stairs to paint some out of reach corner.

* * *

Why do we have to grow up? I remember pushing
button eyes into pastry faces. I remember mittens tied on
with strings, coal eyes, rosy cheeks, and tiny thick coats
cut down from bigger coats. I was happy in red wellies.

* * *

Uncle Juan comes over from Madrid and sits down with
us for a meal, looking ill and disgusted. I think he's going
to throw up, but he just coughs and holds a hanky to his
face. He makes it pretty obvious he finds the place dirty,
and far below his standards. When he wants wire to fix
something, Grandma finds him some garden twine.

Tila mostly stays in her room, but every time she
hears a gunshot from one of the boar hunters she cries
out and tries to drag everyone indoors. It's left to me to
entertain Sergio and the cousins. The bed's filthy. I have
to build a bridge over a gap in the floorboards so the
cousins can get over. I use the *For Sale* house sign from
next door, which grandma has hoarded, and hammer it
in place with some of her odd, assorted nails.

* * *

Grandma's taking Sergio to Juan's for a few days and leaving the dog behind – he's so old I feel so sorry for him. She says some friend's going to come over to feed him but I don't see why she needs to.

I say "I'll take care of him."

She shakes her head and says, "You helping Miguel sell potions, and too busy looking after Tila. She can barely look after herself."

It starts really lashing with rain and I put on an album. The woman has an amazing voice, and I start to sing too. It's about how someone could've apologised, and didn't apologise because they didn't know what they had done. She sings how they could've apologised anyway. I really relate to the song as they are such heartfelt lyrics.

Someone knocks on the door, asking for directions, and I know the place they want – the turning's very near. They say they hadn't realised it was on this shabby working class estate and I say that's insulting and it isn't that at all.

"Different classes of people live here, some own and some rent their houses, you snob."

* * *

I struggle to breathe, like asthma, but think I just have to get away from this place for a while, without Tila knowing, or she'll barricade me in, or some shit.

No one can force Tila to take medication. I can't stand over her and shove it down her neck when she says she doesn't need drugs anymore. She says she can't even get up in the morning when she takes them, but without them she's bonkers.

My mother broke yet another promise when she said she would talk to Tila.

Aaron

Ashish wants to hang around this ridiculous club, with girls flattering the arse off him, admiring his make-up, loving his heels, but I can't stand it and tell him I have to leave. We find an exit, which isn't totally crammed, and Ashish screws up a greasy take-away wrapper, with food still in it, and tosses it up into the air, so it hits my sleeve and makes a good jacket all greasy. I go exaggeratedly ballistic and start laying into him, hitting him and swearing and crying.

He asks me to marry him.

"Ashish, you would make the most beautiful of brides, but I don't think you're going to convince the registry office you're a woman. In case it has escaped your notice, only men and women get married."

"I'm talking about marrying in front of the people who care about us and who we care about. We can make our own vows. You should move in with me now, and then you can make an honest woman of me."

"I'll move in with you, Ashish. It will be good to see if we can stand each other, before making any vows."

* * *

Tila's an exceptional case. I don't invite her over this morning, but she comes over anyway, greets me with a frown, fingers sticky from glue, because she's already making her wedding outfit using leather pieces. She has me go through all my clothes to find more, and I find an old pair of trousers she can cut up, which she stuffs into her bag, before following Ashish into the bathroom.

I hear her telling him, "A real couple just wouldn't

keep their razors and toothbrushes separate," and she crams his in the glass with mine.

During breakfast she suddenly says, "We need to go to choose the diamond."

I say "I don't think we're getting an engagement ring. Besides, everywhere is closed, it's twenty to eight."

Ashish says "Darling, maybe Aaron doesn't have the money in his account to indulge in all the traditions of heterosexual marriage."

* * *

I customise a pack of playing cards for the wedding invites:

Please join Ashish Patten and Aaron Brice for The Wedding Party at 2:30 pm on 18th July 1994. It will be held on Campo de los Almendros. Drinking and dancing will carry on until very late.

Ashish is given wedding presents by his friends from the recording studio, and they bring me one, too. A silver scroll, almost as thin as the silver paper from inside a cigarette packet, with a song title and lyrics written on the reverse. Everyone seems excited to think of us walking off into the sunset.

* * *

The party food is laid out on the grass and, when I open a cardboard container holding eggs, some of them smashed and I wonder if they're okay to use. I make scrambled eggs over the gas stove but Heena says she just wants toast, and as there's a big pile of sliced, crusty bread, I pull them out of the box stuffed with items for the wedding. When I take a carrot stick out of the salad and dip it in ketchup, Heena suddenly freaks out and rushes off. Was some mysterious body horror unleashed with the removal of a salad item and a bit of sauce?

PART FOUR

Poke him and he spurts violence, unwilling to satisfy a world of greater expectation. Nerveless, while others flap, he shakes off emotion like a wet Labrador, talking himself into anything.

Diana

A month or two after I moved into my studio, Catalina's English neighbour, Amanda, held a party to welcome me to the area and introduce me to people. I couldn't see that my arrival would be a cause for celebration. Surely Amanda would consider, 'Artist moves into outbuilding close to my property boundary', to be a misfortune. The first thing she said was, "I got rid of all the old garden furniture and replaced it with the latest and best in light of you coming to join us."

We laughed, though I hadn't understood the joke, and then we ate pear slices. Some funny guy held lettuce up to his ears and did a rabbit impersonation, I assume because all the food laid out was fruit or salad. Hungry still, I split open one of the pomegranates but Amanda's husband, Peter, suddenly appeared from nowhere and took the bowl of pomegranates from the table, and crammed them on a high shelf.

"The pomegranates are Amanda's because she picked the lock to open the gate to the campo."

"How did she pick it?"

"With a piece of rusty wire she found in the field, I think."

"Peter, maybe it was already open and she just pretended to unlock it."

"Maybe."

Amanda, the pomegranate stealer, giggles.

Later, Peter takes his son and puts him on his lap to punish him. He's whacking him with his bare hand in a disturbing fashion.

So much for the ways of the English living abroad. I've tried to avoid them ever since.

* * *

On the grounds of Catalina's villa, I'm overcome by the underlying odour of moss-rot, rubber tyres and inner tubes which have gut-spilled onto the sucking mud at the bottom of her land. I've always had a sense of smell so acute I can smell the sweat as it forms, and sense the salty sea from afar. Close up, someone's perfume enters and overwhelms me. I try to close my nostrils to keep my inner odour intact. Old thoughts – stashed away thoughts – are suddenly dramatically revealed whenever I catch a whiff of scent, and I feel exposed.

I have a sudden desire to drive to the forest, though I'm scared I'll be overwhelmed with memories of the murders. I drive with heat-flushed cheeks, and when I arrive, sit under the mascara-wand trees, taking my time breaking open the bread, and eating it with an olive oil drizzle, and fresh tomato rubbed over it, so it bursts with flavour.

I realise that out here I'm not afraid of anything and could never give up my freedom. Birds peck at the side of the road, and fly up irritably when traffic gets too close. I think of the birds in cages in Granada, and how when I took Heena, she was disgusted and released them, letting them go out of love, following their radical shapes and letting them spread their wings.

She said "Even releasing one's worthwhile. It's always worth saving a life," and then she emptied eight of the cages. She was prevented from opening the ninth by an angry stallholder who pinned her arms behind her back, and threatened to call the police. She sweated inside her PETA approved plastic, but managed to get away. Miguel was wearing his leather jacket because he thought it made him look hard, and as usual this made Heena furious. The forest guards my secret well, a sanctuary from the paranoia which overwhelms me at times.

Today when I get back from the forest I have a reward waiting for me:

Filled With Ghosts

Dearest Diana,

What a nice surprise. I know you won't believe me but I was thinking of you recently. I'll be exhibiting again after a little break, and started to look through the names of artists whom I thought of contacting. Please tell me what you're up to and mail me some photos of your recent art work. I look forward to meeting you again, of course.

Best,

Jan.

* * *

Dear Jan,

The photos I sent you show work made during the last six months. Finally I have my own studio, and I've been summoning the courage to stray and look at life again. Geography and place influence the construction of the paintings.

1 Peyote
2 Metal Studio
3 Clockwork Bullet
4 Labyrinth
5 R and G Map
6 Shotgun Flowers

This series, where the shotgun shells themselves are embedded in wooden doors as painting supports, have developed into a further series where the shotgun shells become a motif. The concept's based on my realisation that more and more people are protecting themselves from an unseen thief or outsider.

I think this is the best work I've ever made, and I'm very excited at the idea of exhibiting with you again.

Yours,

Diana.

* * *

Diana,

   So brave of you, so enterprising. I love your artworks, unrestrained, violent, couldn't possibly have been painted anywhere else. What are your plans for this year? I've just returned from Morocco and will be going there again in March. I'll be in Spain until then and could visit your studio.

   Write please.
   Kisses,
   Jan.

* * *

The ceiling of my studio space is collapsing and shifting. Two large areas are affected – the room where I sleep, and the installation room. Large chunks have fallen, and loose powder is constantly trickling down. I know some of my neighbours, friends of Miguel, have been on the roof and weakened the structure, so eventually the whole roof will cave in. I imagine Miguel set them onto doing it, after a drink and drug fuelled evening and, unlike him, they probably feel some remorse.

* * *

When I stormed into the bar this evening, several neighbours looked down at their feet and shifted uncomfortably. Of course, Miguel didn't miss a beat.

   "You're paranoid. I've done nothing, and I know nothing."

   "Miguel, even during all those years when I loved you, I found it hard to live with your manipulations. I put up with you constantly twisting meanings, circling round me with your waltzing thoughts, spinning your dizzy lines. You disorientated me so much my own stories started to feel like they belonged to someone else."

   Miguel fails to realise I'm no longer that person, I've found an identity which I can rely on.

"Miguel, can't you see why your sabotage and verbal abuse is driving me further away from you rather than back into your bed?"

"Dee, don't throw away opportunity. You never understand the value of what you could possesses, you walk round in ragged circles. The villa could be yours."

* * *

I wrote to Jan again, concerned for my artwork, and the damage the destruction of my studio's causing. I got this reply from her today:

Dearest Diana,

Sorry to read about problems with crazy neighbours. This is getting serious, isn't it? I'm sending you the details of the chap who may be helpful, he's an old hand in Granada's neighbourhoods and knows a few people. Tomorrow I'm sending him a letter saying you'll contact him, just in case.

Be brave.

Kisses,

Jan.

* * *

Jan's friend, Alfonso, knocks on my studio door while I'm drinking a beer and gloomily contemplating my future. Alfonso's an established sculptor and I'm excited to meet him, even if it's under the present circumstances. He's derogatory about the work of many artists showing at present, but full of praise for mine. I tell him I have to move out of my studio because of the problems, and show him how parts of the cave-like ceiling are falling down. He sits under a section of the work.

"You know, it looks amazing, like animal skulls made of stone or horn. I can see it's going to fall down, though. We need to salvage what we can."

Part of the installation involves vessels for containing sacrificial parts and Alfonso removes the description labels, which are sticky and hard to peel off.

Plaster is drifting down near his head and he moves just before some hefty chunks come crashing down. We move outside rapidly, and a bunch of small children gather to watch us. They've clearly been dressed by Pilar, who, as self-elected communist leader of the entire district, has been collecting and re-distributing food and clothes. The children are dressed in a weird collection of traditional clothes, and look like shrunken versions of their parents.

Alfonso finds it hysterical, but I say, "It's okay, they'll be able to change their aesthetic taste on the long journey of life!"

At home, Pilar dresses Sergio in a sheepskin waistcoat, with a jacket over it in a darker sheepskin, which he somehow manages to look really cool in, even during the warmer months.

Alfonso arranges for a van to collect my work and take it to the converted monastery in Cadiz which is his home and gallery space.

Emptying out the studio's only part of the problem; stopping Miguel from continuing the harassment is a bigger issue. I decide to confront him about it and, as I'm walking out of the studio, he turns up at the door and starts talking about an idea Heena has about going to England.

"Stop avoiding the subject, Miguel. I know why you're here. Look at the damage you and your cronies have caused inside my studio, it looks like a quarry, puzzle pieces of ceiling all over the floor, everything I've made covered in white powder."

He's disinterested, and says, "Dee, things always shift a bit in the winter, because of the rain."

He pokes around vaguely and before he leaves, adds, "There's nothing healthy about living among your work. You have a place at the villa. Catalina's gone. I made sure she couldn't come back. I would hate for something to happen to you as well, through your stubbornness."

"Miguel, keep away from me, or I'll get the police involved."

"Dee, you don't want the police here, poking around, asking questions you wouldn't be happy to answer. It's very simple. Move into the villa with me, and no one gets hurt, no one finds out anything."

"You can't stop me involving the police to investigate your vandalism because of your murders. They aren't going to connect the two."

"Maybe I'll decide I want to talk about the murders, reveal you're the killer, stole their car and abandoned it. I can describe exactly where. It couldn't be me who abandoned the car, because I can't drive."

"We both know you'd never go near the police. You're as terrified of the police as Pilar is. You both have records."

"Maybe I'll kill you if you don't come back to me. That would be the easiest solution. I killed Catalina when she tried to leave me, and no one suspected a thing."

I've no idea if Miguel's using Catalina's death as a way to threaten me, or if he was in some way responsible for her accident. I know he didn't directly kill her, because a car mowed her down, and he doesn't drive. But he has cronies, stupid or totally unscrupulous, and with the promise of wealth, no doubt he could've hired someone.

He still fails to grasp that this possibility makes me even more nervous and anxious to get away from him and the villa. This part of my life's over. I know when I leave here I won't ever be coming back, and I feel sad about it.

* * *

I have to throw away pieces of work too damaged by the roof caving in to rescue and store at Alfonso's. I fill the boot of my van with copper and wire costumes, rubber sculptures, and plaster casts, and drive to the dump. I imagine them being uncovered one day in a future archaeological dig, and think how confusing this art will be to future inhabitants. They'll attach strange stories of their own, and maybe project onto them imagined uses, religions, ceremonies.

* * *

I have to say goodbye to so many places and end up walking for miles, taking quite a difficult climb along the cliffs, the tide crashing below. I wear the brown leather pouch I made years ago for my passport while hitching, and it makes me feel braver about striking out on my own. I've done it before, when very young, and can do it again now I'm older.

I pull a loaf of bread out of my pack and light a fire to toast it. For some reason I'm expecting a special kind of slice to appear, some kind of sign that I'm making the right decision, and I toast and eat slice after slice. But they're just ordinary big flat slices and I'm not sure quite what I had been expecting. It's getting late and I realise I can't get home before dark.

Back at my studio, Miguel's waiting on the step. Furious because I haven't let him know I'm leaving; a neighbour informed him. The days when I have to answer to Miguel's demands are over, and I tell him it's none of his business. He demands I remain in the town, and follows me along the street, shouting, "If you leave I'll turn your studio into a pub. The rooms will be knocked together and filled with tables, and outside a swimming pool."

Miguel sweats inside the fur hat he wears, his badge of cruelty. His loneliness is recent and sudden, the fear of dying alone, and he feels the need to surround himself with people. On the street, someone's using a hose to spray the dust from tons of pomegranates piled up on a cart. A neighbour is chatting about all the things that are good in the town, especially the friendliness of the people. I start crying when I think of all the people who are happy with their families and don't have to leave.

I drive to Pilar's house, and I'm excited about seeing everyone, even if it's only the briefest of visits, and even though it's to say goodbye. The door's open onto the terrace but the house is empty. Pilar's neighbours are relaxing in their garden at a big table. They invite me to wait with them, and offer me some wine, and we chat until it starts to feel really late and I can't understand why the others still haven't got back. I look indoors, in case they came in without me noticing, and went straight to bed, but the house is still empty. I'm sure something has happened to them, though when I look at my watch it's only nine thirty.

I look in on Sergio's bedroom. He has pliers and scissors sticking out of a bedside tin, and I don't like that. I think an intruder could grab them and use them against him. For some reason his cot and baby things are set up in the room and I hope Pilar isn't letting him play with dolls, because Miguel would go ballistic. He can't stand any sign Sergio might not be a hundred per cent macho. I feel sad I won't see the children for a long time, and guilty about leaving Tila in the mental state she was in last time I saw her. I intended to have a proper chat with her, but the problems with Miguel trashing my studio intervened, and I think my survival is dependent on me getting away. I've searched for ways of coming back to Pilar's, but it's too risky. Miguel has said he killed Catalina when she tried to leave him, and I can expect the same.

* * *

I haven't been sleeping at night, and am anxious during the day. Miguel's ego is dependent on submission. He doesn't have strangler's hands; they are delicate like a surgeon's, and the same impulse to cut drives him.

I can't risk him finding me here, so I can't hang around any longer and will have to take off without saying goodbye to everyone. I'll find a bed and breakfast place and not let anyone know where I am. I've finally found freedom from my feet of clay and am filling with hopes of transformation. Maybe solutions to problems are overrated; it's more about trying to put things you believe in place.

* * *

I dream:

I'm caring for a child, but realise it can suddenly run fast, and I go tearing after it, but it's out of sight and when I catch up it's sliding face down, down a huge stone staircase. I run to the bottom, where the child's sitting up. I pick it up but it's almost lifeless, just making a slight sound.

* * *

Empty blocks wake up knowing apple-core streets are scratching time. It's as much truth as they can stand. Hot tomato soup sun rises over *Hotel El Gato*, my bed and breakfast accommodation, whose walls, holed by hypodermic-syringes, are reflected in windows smeared with guard-dog slobber.

In *Hotel El Gato*, Kiko, (door on the right), and I are comparing stories of what brought us here. His tablets are dark-pink, bi-convex, oblong, and film-coated. They contain six milligrams of *Risperidone* and he doesn't like to take them.

Behind the door opposite, Maria's fingers fly to knit a purple wrapper to fold around her floppy-headed newborn. She came here when someone kicked the shaved stick propping up her shelter; trampled the stretched gingerbread men whose hand-holding shadows watched her rattle raisins over her cosy fire. Let down by the crumbs of her incessant cooking, Maria's still clutching for a tidy life to cling to.

Down the corridor, Rosa's nailed into a life that doesn't fit. When her love failed to release the clutch of his addiction, her man held it's uselessness against her, and used her beauty as a stick to beat her. Rosa shakes, (spent-match-shaken-in-the-box shakes). Surreptitiously, in the greedy, craving part of my brain, I begin to create hybrid garments; a disguise to clothe new purpose. A hot tomato soup sun may rise over *Hotel El Gato*, but what we learn in the dark will remain with us all our days.

Most evenings I watch TV on Kiko's twelve inch black and white screen. We aren't allowed even a kettle in the room, so I usually bring back takeaway coffees and tapas for us to share.

One evening I get back to *El Gato* to find the woman in the room above me left her taps running and the ceiling's now on the floor of my room, and all my possessions, few though they are, sandwiched between the two. Kiko lends me clothes and when I say how much I like wearing them, he offers to let me keep them. Maria says he had a meltdown when he heard the ceiling crashing down into my room, because he thought I was in there, under the rubble.

* * *

My new room's as awful as the last, though minus the dog-slobbered windows, as it's on the first floor. I won't be able to climb out of the window to assemble on the lawn when one of the residents sets off the fire alarm – which is frequently.

This room's all damp greys. I crave the slatted blinds of my studio, the way they trapped the light and threw it onto the walls with mathematical precision and intuitive grouping. My mystical timepiece, a masterpiece of precision and restrained flamboyance, a contradiction of light and shadow.

I'm nostalgic about those happy yellow days and the mysterious charcoal evenings which mesmerised me for hours. I would sketch the shadow's creeping journey as it signalled daybreak and sunset. I've never felt less inspired than I do in this place, though I think it was Van Gogh who advised looking for light and freedom and to not ponder too deeply over the evil in life.

In my head I'm living Miguel's life at the same time as my own. I've no idea if he'll try to find me, how he'll deal with me if he ever does. Yet, knowing his recklessness when drunk or high, I hope he doesn't commit another crime and risk being caught. He has never shown any remorse for what he did, for what *we* did, and I'm still shocked by the way he treats the murders so casually, because 'homosexual equals corrupt', and therefore has to be extinguished.

I read somewhere the end is already written into the beginning. That seems to let us off too easily, makes us blameless. Even if everything's changed by one decision, even if things are decided before we're aware of them, I'm sure there'll be a price to pay somewhere along the way. Being aware of something means you start to pay attention to it. Is this fuzzy logic?

* * *

I call Pilar, and it's been such a long time it's so good to hear her familiar voice. She tells me all her news and I'm glad to hear Tila's safely in the hospital, though I'm horrified to learn why she ended up there.

When I ring the hospital and ask them to put me through to Tila, I hear her voice but I quickly cut off because I can't really face questions about why I took off, why I've stayed out of contact. She's probably too doped up to think straight, but at least while she remains in hospital she's safe.

I'm expecting Miguel to use his proximity to her as a

threat any day now. What the hell will he be up to? I know too many of his secrets to feel secure.

I call Aaron a few days later, and the first thing he says is I should go to see Tila. She has been released from hospital and is with Miguel. I can't believe she's ended up with him, but I feel partly to blame for leaving when things were really bad for her.

"Aaron, I really don't think Tila would want to see me."

It's impossible to risk my own safety by going near Miguel. Tila might be in danger but I can't give the police a reason to investigate Miguel without ending up in the frame myself.

Overhead, a police helicopter hovers on shabby blades and I imagine it's on the way to pick up Miguel – that the police are here for him. I have a recurring vision of a square hole in the kitchen wall – someone looking through and blowing the whistle. Someone taking everything from him, before he spreads his brand of poverty like a disease – his kingdom of rot exposed. He's so important to himself he thinks he has the right to control other people, and I'm aware that Miguel is capable of disposing of inconvenient people.

Miguel

For the magician, an illusion must always be in place, a veil, some kind of trickery to conjure up what's already there, to make the audience see it. We see what we expect to and when we encounter things in the sensual world we recognise them through seeing, feeling, tasting, smelling, and hearing. We feel secure. But there are things that exist which can't be recognised by the five senses. People who are ill often encounter them, before they are locked away or dulled by prescription drugs.

A young couple come to the door, wanting to meet the great magician. They're on holiday, drunk on absinthe, and pass me the last of the bottle.

"Is anyone else hanging around the place?"

"You mean young acolytes? No, not today," and they invite me for a drink at the nearest bar. I'm suspicious that they're asking me about visitors. Why should they? They may have heard I have certain powers to heal, that people knock on my door for cures, but it's too much of a coincidence they ask such questions when I have Tila with me.

Tila was thankful to be released into my care by the hospital when my mother was unavailable, unreachable by phone. Tila had no option but to stay at the villa, and she's in safe hands.

* * *

I need to know what this pair are up to and that's the only reason I agree to go for a drink with them. They lead the way to their vehicle and I realise it's a familiar car. Why do they have this car? Are these people mocking me? I've always tried to invent a better version of myself, one that pleases more, but I'm also a warrior. If anyone tries to fight me it'll be like fighting a dragon with sugar tongs, my strength and pride would never let them win.

I see the couple touch each other intimately as they get into the car and at that moment the scales drop from my eyes, and I realise they're both men, so corrupted one dresses as a woman.

I've always known how to tease dog fish so they jump right up onto my plate, and these men are fish dangling on the end of my line. If I pull the hook from inside their gullets, they'll be inspired to let out a cry more heart-breaking than a seagull. Their spines, their entrails, will be dragged out of them, as worthless as bait. Black bile will smear their jaws. They look into my eyes, and realise they're waking up to a mistake.

Perhaps they arranged this too: I see a police car pull up and armed officers approach my villa. How did the police find me? Was it this pair of devils, or did Dee hand herself in? I open my wooden coffee box, and take out the silver hand, whose thumb is positioned to ward off the evil eye; a present sent from Greece. What happens next? I would tear my way out but my claws are gone, my fingers numb, instinct shrivelled.

I watch the detectives as they slide the gate, and I know this case will crack open another future. They've come to arrest me. I must take a different path, not tread the same one in all its disguises. It's so clever, life, with all its theatrical makeovers and flourish, managing to look like a new route. It's so seductive, but I have to cover new ground and summon the willpower to look outside myself at what's really going on, not inwards to how it appears.

I'm surprised how glacial the temperature runs, in this blue-veined landscape, like limbs whose track marks tell their own story. Dispersed, I integrate myself into the very brick dust and paint of the distempered walls. My eyes lose their thick glutinous film and become transparent, blue, all-seeing. There's a strip of runway on either side of me, with lanterns lit, and I come upon a roofless palace, ruined, abandoned. When I pull open the door I see limbless creatures, pulling themselves across the floor.

Purple light strains through a crack in the wall, and I climb through to witness a sumptuous feast laid out, all fruit, many I don't recognise. I wonder if I'm the only guest, or if I'm even invited. Faint murmured hums fill the space and I feel a shimmer echo in my bones. I touch a fruit and it collapses, hollow, eaten from within. I realise I'm seeing my own handiwork, this my table of discarded desire, a mocking display.

I forever led women along a gravelly path towards houses whose crackly yellow windows are like greaseproof paper wrapped around loaves. Treacle toffee and toffee apples convinced them it was a carnival and if they crossed my palm with silver I told them their fortune. I revealed their future would only mirror and diminish their past; that in age they'll forget who they are and why. With no more sap, they'll snap when they try to bend in the wind.

There are multiple endings here, with all the paths I didn't take. I've imagined separating and dying in a thousand ways and rehearsals for future endings. I see foamy water that swallows children and pets. Bombs explode and devastate the whole city, with me alone on a bridge above the wasteland, unable to get to anyone. Tanks fill with mossy water and their inhabitants grow until they bust their way out. I'm surrounded by enemies, eaten alive in this savage world of possibility, while a tall man listens to my anger, then walks unscathed through the same brutal crowd.

Peering through the back of my own head, in a circle of golden faces, I watch space evolve into distance, watch the hare cross his feet, and pull apart once more its stomach for my satisfaction. Pressing my hand against my own heart, I feel it beat before plunging my hand into the hare's craving chest. Pulling out the contents and serving them on a bed of lettuce while he watches from his burrow, protecting a thousand more of his species. The carotid artery's an old favourite of mine. This is not distress, it's a creative act, filled with truth. A gentle push of my stiletto into the side of its neck, stir it, and wrench out. It's beautiful and efficient.

Watch.

Pilar

I have dream. Am surrounded by Noah's Ark animals. Tila flood place so no one can get to us. We in big flat boat. She put barricade up, too. We gush out into a corridor. Someone after us and I rush to room and close door. Tila try follow me, but I don't want to let her. I have feeling is her who done something wrong and not me. This dream leave me uneasy feeling on waking, because it seem to tell me something. I always believe dream tell something, but not a good thing.

At the table, Sergio not eat his bread, only want to draw. Start drawing crocodiles, he fill drawing pad with them and ask for another. They very good drawings, goggle eyes and spines along back recede above the water. I ask him where he seen crocodiles look like that and how he draw them so good. He say he have dream, and in dream crocodile show him how.

"Grandma, crocodile told me a bad thing will happen."

Straight away, because of my dream, I think is something with Tila, that she danger, but no idea what she do. Or maybe is she in danger? She keep saying we get hurt. I think maybe I should leave Juan house and go home. Juan say I crazy when I ask him drive me home. Car only crawl along and I frustrated, because now I start to know something very wrong.

When I get home and soon police arrive, I know what happen before they say, "Heena been hit by car."

I not blame Tila out loud, because she had bad time too, and I guilty, because I should stay home not let Heena manage Tila. Heena not hurt, bad, but stitches

121

are hard for a young girl and she tell me she scared to kill baby in fall. I not even know she pregnant, but not end of world. Dee already have Heena when she seventeen, and I used to babies in house, always a good thing, so we manage.

They take Tila to hospital in Granada, and maybe give right drugs she better soon. That girl need help if she think save someone by pull in front of car.

Dee finally ring. I cannot believe she care so little for what happen to us all. Why she take off anyway, she always have home here?

"Dee is time you come home, no stay in bed and breakfast. No one reach you, and you welcome back here. Everyone need you. Heena scars hurt me more than anything. Heena say it not bleed, but Dee, her wound bleed pints, and neighbours run around with wash cloths and towels too. She still deny blood, block memory."

"I didn't know anything about that, Pilar. Is she okay?"

"How anyone tell you anything, when no one hear you for months? I love care for Heena, Sergio, and baby, but Heena sick of Miguel always drag her off for magician, and sick of Tila almost kill her. Why else she take off on hitch-hiking and worry me sick."

"What baby, Pilar? Could no one stop Heena hitching? She's only sixteen."

"She seventeen. You miss her birthday. Miss everything. Your friend Tila in psychiatric hospital now. You send her to me when she sick, and see what happen? You come back, Dee."

"Miguel will hurt me if I go back to your house, Pilar."

"Well, Dee, believe me I know soon enough if he have plan for you, I sit tight. No need alarm yourself about that. You need come home. Maybe Tila out of hospital in week or two, and health precarious. She think she have to kill herself or all her friends and family die.

She terrified for Heena. You and Miguel have problems, but running away not fix. History have habit repeat itself. Come home quick."

Tila

It's about 1.30 pm and everywhere is shut for siesta. I start walking along the pebbly beach and add a razor shell to my collection. They come from Barbados, travelling in the heat inside a fish's belly or trapped inside a mermaid's hair. Salt is sprinkled on their faces.

Picking up shells, we change every one of their plans. Some of them were lashed onto this beach, but some have slowly shuffled their way along the shore like the pottery toadstool inching its way along the path. It's a big responsibility to hear the story. It needs eyes, ears and tongue to unfold.

I don't like the bonfire smell. I pick up the brie and nibble off the rind, the best part. Back come the waves. I sit outside a café, and the manager tries to clear it because something's overheating and threatens to explode, maybe a bottle bomb. I run out and I think everyone else will do the same, but people carry on with their meal.

Crossing over a bridge whose balustrades are uneven rectangles, one comes off in my hand – it's just hollow and hasn't even been cemented. It leaves a big gap in the railings as I stumble down. Someone's talking through a mouthful of white chocolate and I have to take some out with my hand. A huge kite blows away from kids struggling to contain it, and wraps itself around a beach house.

Suddenly, a wave starts along the path, turns into a tidal wave, and sweeps me along the beach. After it passes, I rush through the water and the drained beach, calling for Heena. I think I hear her but I can't find her.

I run into a tiled tunnel, white chunky tiles which start crumbling as if from an earthquake, and I race through it trying to get ahead of the cracking, but I know I can't and I'll be trapped and smothered.

Is this an asylum?

Fears curl, cashew nut pale and subtle, charmless shapes trammel sleep, to make the most of going mad.

Memory dropped in brackish water falls in rotten disturbance as fears curl, cashew nut pale and subtle.

Ticks of unruly childhood are still burrowing and plumping neck-deep to make the most of going mad.

Scars refusing to hold stories are forgotten happenings in suffering places as fears curl, cashew nut pale and subtle.

In the bloodstream of first betrayal, they're ankle-dragged and handed over to make the most of going mad. In the clattering behind the gush, ears shrink in wetness as fears curl, cashew nut pale and subtle, to make the most of going mad.

* * *

A woman just followed me into the toilets – to check I don't escape through the tiny window maybe? She looked under the door to talk to me, and really pissed me off. I didn't want to talk to her.

After I washed my hands, I flung the towel on the floor and walked out. The psychiatrist insists my anger's only the tip of the iceberg, and when I erode that anger, up rises the iceberg; another tip, more anger.

* * *

One of the women gives me two gold earrings, takes them from a drawer with the letters MM scratched into the wood, and I wonder what that means? When she gives me the earrings, it triggers a guilt trip about my mum and I ask if I can ring her.

* * *

Someone says "Oh God, look at this," and shows me a big splashy thing which was cut into my flesh during the night, though I don't remember it happening and it doesn't hurt.

* * *

My bag's full of photos instead of my wallet and money. I remember I asked Aaron to bring me photos from rehearsals, and photos of the books I've read, because I can't remember the titles. But now there's this whole bag of photos.

* * *

We're in a yellowed room, and there's one guy smoking a cigar, so everything's impossible to see through a cloud of smoke. Another guy has his arse practically in my face, so I'm squeezing it, which he obviously likes. I say I'll do whatever he wants in front of everyone, but I won't go off privately. Someone sneezes and it's on my face, wet, just a little.

* * *

Someone picks up a small woman, as if they are a bird with a beak. I go to the market on my own, but wish someone was with me; it's frightening out today. At the market I'm angry when they won't take back a pill box I have only just bought, without noticing chips on its round surfaces. So I smash a load of things on their stall, really go for it.

* * *

One of the women has lost her memory of everyone here, but she has gained an intuition about people she used to know. She can't remember who they are, but she has a memory of how she felt about them, and what kind of person they are. Good at heart or bad inside

* * *

I've seen the limits of my mind, had it scattered across Spain and time. I've burned as a witch, faced the Inquisition, and torture. I've experienced life, whereas the psychiatrist is watery. I can't imagine her fucking.

"Did you keep a diary of your moods this week?"

"I have nothing."

"What made you sad?"

"In the day room everyone rolled over and showed me their underbelly. I wanted to stroke them, to pet them. They were excited, some of them. Desperate for the fuss and the attention. One of them was called Bella, and that made me sad, because she's no beauty. She has a pink belly with tiny nipples, and she snorts, snuffles, a little like a pig."

"Did you say anything to her?"

"I stroked her underbelly, scratched it, and gave her some fuss. Her boyfriend's skinny, glasses, lots of piercings. He's afraid she might jump up at me if she got too excited. Bella wears a pink collar, and in this way announces, 'I'm a beautiful woman', because otherwise no one would suspect it."

"What made you happy?"

"Bella takes the slow lane, letting everyone overtake. She's on a mission, but has all the time in the world and doesn't want to miss a trick. Imagine if she met her fairy godmother and got her three wishes. She needs time to think what those wishes might be, so as not to waste the opportunity. Bella won't roll over for just anyone, but her belly's tattooed with, 'Try me. Try harder. Try again'. By the third glass of wine, she sees everything in primary colours, with everything smelling of classroom chalk and wax crayons melted on radiators."

"What made you angry?"

"Whenever I saw someone sharpen their claws on someone weaker than themselves. Whenever someone pushed around another person. It's not really possible to walk into a room without feeling harmed by other people's intentions."

"Is it possible to see the good side of someone, and focus on that? Everyone has a shadow, but I want you to try to see something other than that."

"You want me to turn a blind eye?"

" I want you to try to see a good intention behind what people are doing. Give them the benefit of the doubt. Did you write your shopping list of things you would like to change?"

Shopping List

apples
man-hunt
torture in neighbour houses
drowning in shallow water
the well
the eyes in the house
the bones
the red hot metals
the 2d pictures which were 3d

Someone's doing something outside the door. Thick purple dye is entering the room. I think it'll get on the patterned duvet. A young guy pokes his head around and says there's nothing he can do, it's impossible to clean everything, and his mother has given up trying.

Aaron has brought me a box of fortune cookies. He believes wholeheartedly in cookie wisdom: "Do not stray down paths without something to guide you."

"There's no going back."

"Tila, you know I am always guided by desire. Wanting something's the incentive, but not necessarily a good guide."

"Aaron, follow your breath, follow the scent. Raisins will guide you. Follow yellow things. It doesn't have to make sense."

To get the prediction from your fortune cookie, you usually have to snap it in half, though occasionally a little tag of paper shows, and you can pick it out and read it without cracking the shell. That's a cheat, and the satisfying crack's the whole deal.

* * *

My dream:

I'm walking across a field, and when I start to run the other way a boy asks why, and I say, 'The rich are coming.' There's an amazing image of a flooded road, and being right next to a fox hunt. The rich are all there and have lost the fox. They don't know how to behave in the traffic. One woman has to be pulled off the road when a huge lorry arrives. They just stand there. One of the pompous hunters is ordering someone to close a hatch in the water-filled road.

* * *

I have no idea how I came to be involved in my present life. There's no way of grasping time and to know how long something's going on outside your own mind. Can anyone be sure that their past actually happened? Why else do we keep mementos other than to tie down fragments of the past, to weight them down? Evidence this isn't an invention of the night? I have a tin trunk of souvenirs, but it could be destroyed by now and I'm not sure if that matters.

Do I still need indifference tablets to make me indifferent?

Today they told me that they're releasing me from the hospital. I'll continue to see the psychiatrist, continue to take my drugs, and all I need to do to be back with my family is to prove I have family. This isn't an easy challenge. I can't think of a single person other than Pilar who hasn't let me down. When they can't reach her, and I tell them Miguel's address, I don't imagine he'll bother to pick me up, but he does.

Heena

4 am: A strange journey, which I've kept just under the surface of remembering. I pull a cushion away from the easel where someone's leaning, to paint the man, who's only fragments. His arm was once injured, but he carries on pretending it still is, long after it's healed. I'm looking after a baby. I have to carry it and am trying to get it to hold on in that way which makes it light.

Hitching, I got to know so many people and at times I was amazed at their stories. This was the first time I hitched and felt what it's like to be free of everything. The freedom of having nothing. It makes you seed yourself into the very fabric of the planet. I spent hours alone with my thoughts through sleepless nights, lying on my back, stars seeming only inches from the ant-filled earth. After a while the ants didn't come near me, once I overcame my fear they no longer smelt it. To overcome a phobia you have to put yourself amongst it, face it, and get past it.

* * *

I bought a pregnancy test and after I peed on it, poured a bottle of water on the little stick, because there was no running water. When I saw it was positive I still didn't believe it, and thought maybe it was a false result, because I didn't rinse off the stick properly.

The thought of going back to grandma's makes me claustrophobic and fearful, but my face is puffed up like bitter meat. If only I could shed my skin, have room to grow. I want lightness back, I remember that's how to win.

* * *

Back from my travels, I go to the writing group which mum's friend, Amanda, runs for the ex-pats. We read out our stuff. Amanda leans over me to tell the woman on my other side how much she enjoyed what she has just read out. They exchange cosy details and discuss a storytelling group.

Then she sits back and says to me, "Do you write?"

No, lady, this thing I'm doing here is putting up shelves. This isn't a fucking pen - it's a hammer.

I write down what I can't say to people. I write to avoid intimacy. I write things which, if I said them, would be thrown back in my face, either at the time, or at a later date. My words turned back on me, my own weapon used against me.

New Skin

The *Singer* sewing machine creaks in the corner, hanging over me like a magpie, as she tries to sew me back into my skin to stop me growing. Hanging over me like a magpie, she'll crick her neck to stop me growing. Following the example of her mother, the *Singer* creaks in the corner.

Leaving behind the useful damp in crumpled wet pale milky gleam I seek heat to sharpen the teeth of my new skin. In crumpled wet pale milky gleam I emerge wearing it, the teeth of my new skin, the brighter golden sheen. I emerge wearing it. I seek heat to sharpen the brighter golden sheen, leaving behind the useful damp.

We all want to tell our story and be fascinated by ourselves. I don't like someone more because they've done this or that, been here and there, but somehow I think when I tell others I've been there, or done this, it'll make them understand me more. It doesn't happen like that, they just accuse me of being self-absorbed and disinterested in them. My intention really isn't to compete. But what the hell, if they don't like me there's nothing I can do about it.

I imagine starving this foetus, so it hungers and dies, and when I'm lighter, step out with my light bones showing, to run away so I don't get trapped. Except, I can't run away from this because I'm carrying it inside me. Suddenly, the whole road ripples and buckles and then collapses like a pack of cards and catapults huge bricks from yellow houses into a heap of devastation.

Walking through the children's park, the unfolding concrete paths and railings are like a treasure trail, and I want childhood back. Even a difficult one like mine's better than this. I watch the joy in Sergio's muscles as he lets off steam, releasing energy before it bursts him. I struggle to summon the energy to raise one foot. I feel poisoned and my cells protest. The smell of a bonfire makes me sick, and so does thinking about butter and cheese together on a slice of bread.

I imagine what it would be like, living with Francisco, but when he comes to meet me on his bike and asks why I won't sit on the handlebars, I don't tell him I'm pregnant. It would never occur to him that I am because we only had sex once. I find it impossible to tell him he's going to be a father. His girlfriend Rachel thinks I'm a complete idiot, and mocks me.

The only thing I want to eat is aniseed balls and the only thing I can wear are men's long johns, which I dye pink and orange, with black spots. The bump grows like an egg. But concealed under a big knitted turquoise jumper, no one notices it.

Bad moods strike so suddenly and uncontrollably. Back at Grandma's house, I throw every one of my possessions out of the window. I also throw chairs around, and feel the baby inside protest at my exertions.

Late at night I go around to mum's studio, but no one's in, and notice a window's smashed and then realise it isn't the right building. I go back to the street, hail a cop car, and say I need taking home. The baby goes quiet and still for more than a day, and I think I've killed him.

When I tell grandma I'm pregnant, she starts to knit a blue jumper because she's sure it's a boy and talks about how we can paint stencils on the walls of the box room. She hunts out a crib and finds pram wheels, which almost fit though the crib slides backwards and forwards a bit.

My clumsy bulk causes me to break a figurine, which is very precious to her. She isn't upset, but I burst into tears when it happens. It's not something you can mend with super glue.

I have a scary dream, with all sorts of supernatural events. There are footprints and floods and noises. There's a gang of us. We are all terrified. I'm with a woman and running down a slope and suddenly the sea's rushing towards me, and great waves are going over me. I don't want to go back to where I've come from. I remember a fragment with a huge book, the pages loose and in the wrong order. I remember seeing page six.

At one-thirty I'm watching TV with Pilar, when the first contractions of my stomach muscles hit as gently as a jackhammer. At three-thirty, we're in a cab racing towards Granada Hospital.

"Narrow hips," has never been said more accusingly as I'm held back, doggy-style, from crawling off the table and escaping full-bellied.

At eleven-thirty the following morning, in a release of pain and ecstasy, and with the sound of wet fish hitting the decks, my tiny boy's born. He seems to be wearing electric-blue skin socks, and clings to me like a limpet. We're five floors up in a glass-fronted cell, but there's a rainbow outside.

The midwife strokes my hair, tells me I'm a brave girl and have a beautiful baby. He looks like the longest baby imaginable as they put him in a little cot.

I have my newborn in my arms, walking down the corridor, and I fall forward and can't use my hands to save myself. So my knees slam against the ground, and a woman takes my baby from my arms and I stagger to my feet, following her down the corridor. She's ahead of me, not acknowledging me, and I think, *Am I mad? Is that even my baby? How can I ask for it back?*

Aaron

I visit Tila in the psychiatric hospital and she doesn't move when I enter the room and sit opposite her. Her speech is slow and heavy.

"Tila, they said there was an accident. I'm so sorry."

"I tried to save Heena. I'm a coward. I didn't die and her suffering goes on."

"Who told you she's suffering?"

"I hear her screaming in the next house."

"No one's hurting her."

"How could they hunt down a girl?"

"She'll be fine, she's probably staying at Los Almendros. You know Pilar doesn't answer her phone. Either that or she'll be at the villa with Miguel, bottling his medicines."

"I hear screaming from the house next door. Aaron, you have to go and find her. Bring her to see me."

"I'll go to see her and I can tell her you're here. She'll be glad you're finally getting help. I can easily persuade Ashish to go with me, we can have a road trip. It'll be the perfect excuse for a holiday."

"Women go in the house with mops and buckets to wash away the blood."

"To wash away imaginary dirt. This is rural Spain. The women mop."

* * *

We're very stoned and on the way to find Heena. I start thinking about knives, and as Ashish idly turns the pages of a magazine, he announces all the pages have been slashed. Everything washes over me in paranoid blue waves and I have to either ride with it, or ride over it.

"Aaron, look at that sign. It says 'drunken ass'."

Suddenly, our car has mounted the pavement and is going towards people and it almost runs them down. Everyone gasps. The brake fluid case cracked on my *Triumph Herald*, and we hurtle through traffic lights, which miraculously turn green. It's a virtually unstoppable beast, and handbrake, gear change, levelling of road, and clipping a stationary taxi don't halt it. Our car veers across the road and then tips over against a shop. Ashish climbs out because someone's yelling, "Please climb out of the vehicle."

Our car is virtually unscathed, its beautiful chrome bumper just a little dented, but the cab driver wants to kill me. He leaps out of his cab and screams that I'm a fucking queer. Apparently my recently bleached hair is all it takes to prove this. My nervous giggles, a mixture of relief at not being dead, or killing anyone, added to the sight of his ridiculous flamboyant anger, don't help my cause.

We don't wait around for police to arrive, because no one's hurt and, no doubt, the taxi driver would want to satisfy himself with a massive insurance claim for his non-existent injuries. Some doctor would be summoned to pronounce he's hereafter prevented from enjoying watching his beloved football, though obviously no harm to his macho sex life.

We give a lift to a group of rockers who show us where there are swimming ponds to swim naked. It's such a fantastic feeling, jumping in and swimming underwater and it's fun checking out all the cocks.

"Aaron, here's a huge one, tattooed with hot chilli peppers."

I get completely turned on and pop up right next to the gay bar. Ashish offers me some food, but before I eat I want to pee. The toilets are disgusting and shared between men and women. No doors. Some girls come in while I'm peeing and one taunts me that I have no ass. Someone has been accused of drowning a baby.

"You guys should hang around here for a while. There's a town nearby with New Agers, a lot of cool people."

* * *

This is what drunk boys do: we pour cider on each other's backs, and then one of us climbs on the back of a 750 *Kawasaki* motorbike with a man we scarcely know.

I'm kidnapped, driven for miles without an opportunity to climb down. The guy suddenly pulls right across the road and skids to a stop in the hilly place. He kisses me and tells me I have amazing lips, before driving me back to the ponds. I sprawl next to some woman with five tiny kids, and she starts talking about the others she intends to have. Her bloke says they're arguing about it and he's on the verge of leaving. She glares at him and scoops up an armful of kids.

I hear someone say, "Where's the Paki who was here?" as I'm spreading a towel and, for a moment, I think they mean Ashish, because he gets that racist shit. I turn around with my fist raised, but they've dived into the pool. I pull on my red jeans and join the food queue; well I push in at the front, taller than everyone else.

Some guy says "So how are you, Aaron? I haven't seen you since October."

I don't have a clue who he is, and mutter, "Who are you, man?"

He tells me "You don't need to pretend you don't know me. You remembered to swallow when I came in your mouth."

The thought of him lies like oily eggs in the base of my stomach, rising and falling with every step I take away from him. Aversion.

A boy needs a glass and mine's the last one on the

table. He's sexy, I don't want to refuse him, so I pour my red wine onto a plate, for later. The table's a little tipped so it spills off the other side and soaks into the cloth. The waitress says I have to pay six euros for cleaning and asks if I have it. I laugh in her face and say no.

"I don't know how you going to survive without money."

When I get back to the ponds, Ashish is totally unconcerned by my absence, pre-occupied with trying to work out which way around his rubber dress goes back on.

He says "It could be this way, though to be honest it's a bit macho for me, with this rubber tie and collar hanging at the front. How about we go to the *Church with Intent* this evening? It's Indian, I think."

"Ashish, of course we'll go. First we have to go to find Heena. I promised Tila I would, and it shouldn't be hard. Heena will be staying with her dad or her grandma. Let's see how fast I can get this heap of junk to go."

El Monde

A police investigation began.

ND - #0509 - 270225 - C0 - 203/127/12 - PB - 9781909129771 - Gloss Lamination